Rooster

Pemmican Publications gratefully acknowledges the assistance accorded to its publishing program by the Manitoba Arts Council, the Province of Manitoba – Department of Culture, Heritage and Tourism, Canada Council for the Arts and Canadian Heritage – Book Publishing Industry Development Program.

Printed and Bound in Canada.
First printing: 2011

Library and Archives Canada Cataloguing in Publication

Thompson, T. D. (Twila Dawn) 1953-
    Rooster / T.D. Thompson.

ISBN 978-1-894717-64-9

    I. Title.

PS8639.H643R66 2011   C813'.6   C2011-904983-X

PEMMICAN
PUBLICATIONS
INC.
Committed to the promotion of Metis culture and heritage

150 Henry Ave., Winnipeg, Manitoba,
R3B 0J7 Canada
www.pemmican.mb.ca

 Canadian   Patrimoine
Heritage   canadien

 Canada Council   Conseil des Arts
for the Arts   du Canada

Rooster

T.D. Thompson

Twila Thompson

Jan. 2013

For family and friends, whose support and generosity make every day a good day

1

First there were only the clouds. Billowing and huge, they rolled skyward in enormous glowering swells that gleamed silver-white in their curling upper summits. Churning constantly, the clouds' tempestuous undersides swooped with a rowdy energy, silently whipping themselves up, and up, and up again, into swelling crests. A distant blue sky peered out beyond, but my attention was focused entirely on the roiling activity of the massive cloud formations.

I was alone in a vast landscape, high on a remote mountain peak. Steam-coloured cloud swirled in a twisting dance around and over my head and body. Strands of it wound silkily across my arms and spun slowly to cling around my legs. Warm, soothing, and vaporous, the haze at first felt like a comforting hug.

Distant indistinct voices murmured and sighed through the air behind and around where I stood. Their muttered words trailed out in thin bits of laughter and whispered warnings, but I was unable to see who spoke.

My eyes strained in a futile effort to peer through the eerie white film that continued to revolve and shift in a snaky rhythm around me. I was frustrated at my failure to make out anything through the enveloping cloud-form, where I could sense, but not quite see, the other beings that surrounded me, crowding me, swarming around me.

Shadowy figures clung somewhere close in the haze, not actually visible, but not invisible either; portions of an arm, a hand, an ear, appeared and then disappeared back into the surrounding cloud. The forms reached out to me and chilly fingertips trailed softly across my face and over my bare arms.

Someone's cool breath blew over my cheek and lifted my hair. Voices quietly whispered and hissed in my ears. The voices moaned as they spoke to me about important things I couldn't quite hear. There were people I knew I desperately wanted to see and talk to, but I was prevented from doing so by the thick, slithering fierce and untamable clouds.

The ground under my bare feet was flinty and hard. Sharp spears of granite stabbed at my toes and rasped the tender skin of my soles, although, looking down, I couldn't see the rock where I stood. Only my upper legs were faintly visible, disappearing into the mist. The cloudy haze had thickened, becoming heavy and sticky, almost like a dense spiderweb, beginning to stick to my jacket. The fog was denser and no longer just filmy, but textured, like very pale, very thin cloth. It choked the air and began to block my breathing. I could almost taste it.

And then suddenly the sky cracked open. A huge white bird loomed above. The bird's wings beat hard and fast and his breast strained with effort. I couldn't see a beak or eyes, but I could hear and see the wings as they flapped dully, plunging into the foggy air, straining and thudding, like a distant drum beating in a remote pulse.

Feathers drifted down around me. Only one or two at first, twisting lazily down, then more until, as they accumulated, they transformed into clouds themselves. The feathers were white, soft and fluffy, and they were warm. They settled on my upturned face. Their touch at first was soft, like a delicate breath of silky air, like a kiss, on my cheeks and forehead. The downy feathers lay on me, trembling slightly in the breeze, while the enormous bird still hovered overhead, struggling mightily to push its heavy body forward.

Then the drifting feathers began losing their warmth and started to feel cold as they fell in larger wads. They became icy. They filled my nose and ears. I dropped my head to avoid the freezing chill of the things, but they stuck to my eyes, clogging my nose and plugging my ears. I threw my head back and opened my mouth to scream, and jagged freezing feathers immediately filled it. I was choking, unable to breathe or swallow. I tried to spit the things out, but they stuck inside my mouth, jamming up my throat, clumping in a solid mass at the back of my tongue, gagging me.

My hands were clamped at my sides, my fingers stiff and frozen into claw-shapes, and although I strained with every muscle, it was impossible to raise my arms, impossible to use my hands to scoop at the feathers as they drowned me. The barbs now were steely hard, with snapping points that stung where they touched, and they dropped down hard in huge irregular clumps of what felt like chunks of ice.

Frantic now, I tried to run, but my legs were a solid mass of frozen flesh, hard and unforgiving. My arms were trapped at my side, inflexible. I was lost somewhere alone and I couldn't wake myself, or call for help, or make my body obey. My feet were like lead weights, somehow bonded to the rocky earth.

The world was devoid of colour and the air was thicker, harsher, no longer cloudy or comforting. Only frozen blank white. Barren. Devoid of any emotion. Deadly silent except for the drumming of the massive bird's wings.

Inside my head I could hear myself shrieking, but even as I screamed for help, I knew nobody else could hear. Nobody could see me. I was invisible in all the white, covered like a feathered ghost, lost in the colourless terrain. Gone. Gone forever.

Jutting up in bed, I woke with the shock of a hammering heart. The blood pounding through my body echoed the drumming of the enormous bird's wings. My face and upper body were dripping wet with sweat, my breath coming in gasps as I gulped in the air I'd been denied before. Alive! It was so good to be alive. Every breath was sweeter than the one before.

I lay there, gasping and cold, willing my heart to calm down, unsure of where I was until finally my eyes found focus in the dark and the everyday shapes of my bedroom and its furniture became clearer to me, calming me slowly with their familiarity. My hands trembled still with the force of my previous panic. Using the edge of my sheet, I wiped at the cold sweat covering my forehead and cheeks.

Lying there, I was not only afraid to move but also too freaked out to close my eyes again, afraid the dream might come back. Confused by the panic I'd felt, I stared at the outlines of my mirror and dresser where they stood, gleaming silver in the dully reflected lamplight off the street, willing myself to overcome the heavy feeling of dread sitting like a weight on my chest.

As the night slowly gave way to early morning light, and a couple of piles of dirty clothes loomed in lumpy, reassuring hills on the floor, I could see the spines of books I'd left piled next to my computer on the desk, and with the sight of recognizable things the chill finally began to leave me.

My room. I've never been so glad to see anything before in my life.

2

"Dreams happen," Mom rasped next morning. She cleared her throat with a harsh, scratchy cough. "Get over it."

We were bumping into each other in the kitchen in our usual early-morning routine. I dumped cereal into a bowl and she poured another cup of strong black coffee, heavy with sugar.

She was late again, doing up buttons, running around trying to get ready for work. This was never a good time of day to start a conversation with her for a whole whack of reasons, one of them being how she's definitely not a morning person even on the best of days. After her crying jag last night in the living room I should've known better, but I couldn't seem to stop myself from talking about it.

"This was no dream," I insisted.

The experience, the dream, the whatever-it-was, still felt so incredibly potent, it was as if the experience was demanding me to tell somebody. To lessen its horror by sharing. The night's icy, choking sensation of being unable to breathe and unable to yell for help was so strong and real it was almost another presence in the room. I'd been trying to describe it to her, but I was getting nowhere.

Overriding my frustration, I tried again. "This was *real*, Mom. I was really there. I was on a high, cloudy mountain peak someplace. I don't know where it was. And I was being drowned in white stuff. Not snow exactly. Feathers or something weird like that, but they were pointy and cold. They were in my mouth. I felt like I was dying."

The emotions conjured up by whatever happened to me had not gone away with morning light. In fact, in some ways they were stronger now in the daylight than they had been last night, when I lay there for hours unable to sleep again, too afraid to close my eyes. I was still really freaked. Completely shaken by what happened. It was definitely no dream. I'd really been there and I'd been one step away from vanishing forever. My voice was shaky with the remembrance of it all, and in her eyes I could see her annoyance at me and at what she saw as my feeble attempts at explaining it to her.

"It was *terrifying*." I said it loudly, but the word was too weak to actually express what I still was experiencing, hours after the dream ended. There was a shiver skirling up my spine that wouldn't go away.

She tossed back a Tylenol and took another swig of coffee, her eyes half-shut against the morning light.

"James," she moaned, "I don't have time for this. My head's killing me. Just go to school, OK? Maybe we can talk tonight."

But I knew we wouldn't. Tonight she'd be too tired, or she'd park herself in front of the TV with a drink, or she'd head out to the casino to try to make back what she lost last week. Same old stuff.

"Mom," I tried again, seemingly unable to let it go, "this was so freakin' eerie. So weird." I couldn't find the words to describe it to her and, frustrated, I banged the flat of my hand on the counter, making her coffee jump in its cup. "It was real!"

"James!" She turned on me, lips quivering, tears on the way. "Stop it! Just stop! Everybody has dreams, and sometimes they're scary. Knock it off. You're getting too big for this kind of crap. Go to school and leave me alone. My head," she moaned again, "my head is killing me."

Yeah, I thought, well a bottle by yourself in front of the tube can do that to you. But I knew better than to try telling her my thoughts about her behaviour.

Dragging my backpack over one shoulder and leaving my half-empty bowl on the counter, I slammed through the kitchen door, making sure it banged shut hard behind me. Making a point. Making it hurt.

Once outside, I propped myself up against the side of the house to wait for Frank. I was still aware of every breath, like I had been when

I woke up from that weird dream, and the morning air was sweet and cold in my lungs. The little breeze smelled like snow and suddenly with that realization, the air was no longer sweet, but threatening instead. I could almost feel those pointy shards jamming my throat again, filling my eye sockets so I was nearly blinded by them. I hated that damn dream. The dream that wasn't a dream. That was what infuriated me most: how could it have been real like that? Dreams are something you laugh at next morning, something you ignore. Scary clowns, failing tests, stuff like that. What happened to me was absolutely not a dream; of that I was certain.

The morning air was damp and frosty, in the first hint that snow was on its way. Normally, the idea of fresh snow on the way would have got me totally pumped, thinking about Jasper tomorrow and skiing up in the Rockies. The trip we had planned for the upcoming weekend was gonna be so sweet. I'd been watching the weather for the past month and checking every day on the weather sites. The reports said there was lots of new snow up there in the higher elevations already, with more expected over the next few days. Perfect.

All our supplies were ready and we'd hashed everything over in endless detail, partly because we wanted to be totally supplied and didn't want to forget anything obvious, but also because none of us could stop thinking how cool it was gonna be and how much fun we intended to have up there. We had a little dome tent and down-filled bags guaranteed good to -45 so we'd be warm at night, and the three of us were wild about the thought of how beautiful the backcountry and skiing were going to be in all that powder. Cross-country in the Rockies. Best exercise and most beautiful scenery in the world.

Anticipating the trip didn't feel so great today, though. Today, the thought of falling snow only creeped me out.

I still didn't know what had happened the night before, but today for some reason, just being alive seemed like a totally new concept—one I'd never appreciated before. Being able to suck in air was like a gift. I breathed in deep again, trying to recapture my normal sensation of enjoying the icy, humid smell of snow, and began trying to fight my way through the fears and resentment.

The anger I still felt at Mom's reaction, or more precisely, her non-reaction, was typical of my mornings these days. There was a time we'd got along really well, Mom and me. She was young, blonde, pretty and fun in those days. When I was little she'd take me to the playground and sit on the swing next to mine, and we'd have races to see who went highest, fastest. There were pictures of her in jean shorts and a T-shirt and me, laughing in little runners, bare-chested in a pair of too-large kids' overalls, so I knew it wasn't just wishful thinking. It wasn't my imagination. We'd really been that close.

It's always been just the two of us, plus or minus a boyfriend when she had one in her life, and we'd been a tight unit for a long time. It was one of those boyfriends, a guy named Gary, a guy who'd hung around longer than most of them, who had taught me to camp back when I was a kid. Took me to the mountains, showed me how to build a proper fire and how to cook eggs and bacon over it. Inaugurated me into the blessings of hot, sugary tea sipped around a campfire after dark when the stars were so plentiful and so bright in the soft black endless night it felt like they were pressing down on you.

Gary's the one who taught me how and when to change the oil in the old beater he drove, how to check a car's brakes and fluid levels. He showed me how to cut the grass so the lawn had stripes on it, and gave me ways to talk back to the tough guys in school to get them off my case. Gave me tips on pleasing the girls and talking nice to teachers. He was a pretty good guy.

Not her type, she'd said when she turfed him out and it became just the two of us again. I like it better just you and me, kid, she'd said, watching him pack his old car and drive away. Those days were years ago now and it was hard trying to figure out where and when things had gone so far south it was more like she hated me than loved me.

When I was little, it seemed my looking different from her hadn't bothered Mom. At least, she never let on. It's only the last couple of years that I've noticed how she doesn't have time or patience anymore, how she's pulling herself into herself. And I think it's because I look more like him now. I'm not that cute little boy on a swing anymore. I'm 17—shaving, growing, changing. I'm tall and skinny with long arms and huge feet and my nose is too big for my face. Now when I look in the mirror, I have the same eyes and mouth as he did and my skin's the same brown as his skin. It annoys her. She's still pissed at him after all these years.

And that bugs me. I mean, why let it still get to you? Why not move on with your life? What'd he do that was so awful anyway? He got her pregnant with me, but she says they were in love, so obviously he didn't force her or anything. Then what he did was he left. Left her alone to have me and raise me. He left and she's never forgiven him.

And now I look like him, or at least like the few pictures she's still got of him, so I guess my appearance reminds her I'm also Cree and not just descended from Scottish farmers like she is. I'm never gonna be blond or red-haired and freckled. Maybe she thinks I'm polluted by his blood.

I look like an Indian, and for me every day is a lesson in being judged by appearance. Powwow time, baby! Feathers, hoops and beads. Which is ridiculous, obviously, because I grew up in the sub-urbs of Edmonton, a great wide prairie city, not on a reservation or in a teepee. But skin colour is all anyone sees, especially at first. When we study this stuff in school, the rest of the class looks at me and sees "Aboriginal" or "Native." Then we go on in the books and they see "part Cree." And then "Metis." Depends on where we are in studying Canada's history.

But what I am, is me. Only me. James Elroy Campbell. 'Rooster'. And I'm cool with that.

"Hey, Roos-man! Rooster!"

The sound of Frank's hollering finally broke through the fog in my head and I turned to the sidewalk running past our house where he stood jiggling one leg and grinning impatiently at me. Frank Banks was the only guy I knew who actually wanted to stand out in a crowd, no matter what the cost, no matter how not cool, and today was no exception.

Enormous floppy red mitts dangled almost to his knees. A girl he dated for about two weeks, a long haul for him, had knitted them for him, and even though the two of them broke up and the mitts were miles too big, he still wore them. Today, just in case he didn't look weird enough, he'd added a multi-coloured striped hat that dipped down over his ears. The hat ended in a long skinny tail covered with tiny silver bells. It draped over his shoulder like a deflated balloon. He was dressed like a dope and had an even dopier grin on his face. The sparse little moustache he'd been babying along all winter was frosted up from the humidity in the cold air. It was growing out even redder than the hair on his head, and now little ruddy icicles hung on his upper lip.

He's always been skinny, but the older he gets, the knobbier he seems to become. His knees are always poking through his jeans, in a look that he's chosen to think is provocative and lures the ladies. It's my opinion they feel sorry for him. And he's become klutzier than ever, if that's even possible. He's been known to trip and fall over an imaginary rock on the path. We've been friends since the first day we saw each other at some pre-kindergarten deal when we were about three years old. He walked across the room and punched me in the arm and since then it's been 14 years of trying to stay even in the smacking-each-other-around department.

All our lives we were a tribe of two. Kids on bikes with hockey sticks, playing 'hock-olo,' a version of hockey and polo we invented and then played for years, because a game cooler than ours didn't exist. We wanted to be either cowboys or hockey players when we grew up, and we figured as soon as we got old enough to leave home, we'd head out to a ranch and find work. How we figured any sane rancher would want a couple of guys who were hock-olo experts to ride his horses and herd his cattle was a detail we hadn't bothered to work out.

"Ready, buddy?" he asked. "Got your junk together for tonight?"

"Yeah, no. Not yet." I tried grinning back at him, but that bird, that awful vision, kept coming into my head. It was like a never-ending echo. It wouldn't let go. I heard myself say, "I might not go, man."

"Whaaat?" The word was a long-drawn sigh of exasperation. He glared at me and smacked his mitts on his legs. Even his hat seemed to droop.

Frank has a short fuse, and this was the first step toward him blowing up, stomping, hitting the air and yelling. Since I've known him he's been this way. Subject to temper tantrums. Which is ridiculous, because he's almost 17, only a couple months younger than me, and has his own car. A guy with his own car should've outgrown this crap.

"Why the hell not?" His voice rose to danger pitch. "What's up? Did your old lady go nuts again? Ground you again like last summer?"

I joined him on the sidewalk and we started tramping through the icy slush toward the end of the block, where we'd catch the downtown bus and head off together to the arts-oriented school we both attended. I'd fought the whole idea two years ago when Mom enrolled me, but it was a battle I lost before I even knew it was a battle. Her mind was made up; I was gonna get what she figured was a liberal education.

I sure never thought of myself as 'artistic' in any way. In my eyes it was a lot more interesting to knock around on the basketball court, figuring new ways of deking people out, and I'd assumed an arts school would be full of boring arts-farts who spent their downtime making up new steps to old tunes or sketching fruit bowls. I also realized we'd still have to learn all the regular science and math anyway, so why not stay closer to home. Why go all that way just to get fed the same old stuff? Why not just hang here in the neighbourhood where I'd always gone to school? She'd had an answer to everything, and as it turned out, she'd been right. The school was old and decrepit and had a crazy mix of kids, but it was interesting, and when they encouraged me to join a little blues band there, I'd discovered bass guitar. I stunk at it, but I liked it and I liked the shop crafts classes. And the girls. The girls were cool. Frank had followed me there, three months into his first semester at the local high school.

"Frankie," I tried kidding him, using his childhood name, "you and Jen can still go. I'll trust you with her."

He slugged my arm hard, making me slip on the slick sidewalk and nearly fall into a bank of shovelled snow. Catching me off-balance, he flipped the fedora off my head and onto the bank.

"Hey! Not my new one. You bent the feather!" I was kidding, and not kidding. Annoyed, but feeling guilty about being annoyed.

He had bent the feather, but it was a small bend that could be bent back. My fedoras are my thing. They set me apart. It's the feather in my fedoras that got me my name, "Rooster." My 'preferred form of address,' as Jen calls it.

"So you 'trust' me," Frank repeated. "Yeah, sure! As if she'd go with just me. Why aren't you coming?" He assumed a tone of exaggerated patience, as if speaking to a kid with a very limited attention span. "We have all these plans. Remember? Remember our plans, Roos-man? We're gonna ski the back slope of Mount Hesker and then make a fire and cook some smokies. You like smokies! You can put ketchup on yours!" Then he smacked my arm, hard, and hollered, "Where we hiked last summer! It's gonna be awesome! And now you go and wreck it all. What's up, man?"

"I don't know." I dusted the snow off the brim of my hat and shoved it back on. It didn't really keep my head warm, but it looked cool and that's what mattered. I felt unfinished, raw, without my hat.

"Just don't think I want to anymore," I finally answered lamely.

We were at the bus stop. And of course the connector bus that would deliver us to the rapid transit train that would then deliver us to a station a block from school, was nowhere in sight. We shivered as we waited, stamping our feet and shoving our hands in our armpits—the story of my life in this country, it sometimes seemed. Even summer is cold a lot of the time here in Alberta. The only thing we all agree on in this part of the world is that the weather is mostly terrible, always unpredictable and too dry, too wet, too hot or too cold.

"Jen'll still go with you," I tried to soothe. The words came out in a breath of foggy air. "She likes you."

"Ha!" he sulked.

"No really, she likes you like a brother," I insisted. "A little brother. One who needs guidance and help and the advice of a big sister. She likes you like that." I couldn't stop a grin. "She thinks you're perfect. Perfect for somebody else."

He hauled off, but this time I ducked and avoided his fist.

"Perfect for somebody she's not that crazy about," I continued. It was a relief to just knock around and forget last night's dream.

"Perfectly imperfect," I finished as the bus rolled up and I followed him on.

Frank kicked out at me, and the balding, big-nosed driver gave us both a glare. Business as usual.

3

It was on Sunday afternoon when seemingly all the crap in the world hit the fan. That's when my life as it had always been spun completely out of control. That's when I began to want more than anything else to somehow turn back the days. Turn back the clock. Stop time and then reverse it. Make it all un-happen.

But on that Friday morning, when Frank finally grabbed me in the hall and forced me to tell Jen I was crapping out of the trip, I only knew that because of my dream experience I was too uneasy and junked-up to possibly go with them. I had a headache that would kill a horse. My throat was raw. It'd wreck the trip if I went, and I could see even while explaining it to her as reasonably as possible, Jen was completely ticked. She gets that way often, and even though it's one of the things I like about her, that she's able to tell me off once in a while, I was still annoyed with how she didn't seem to want to understand how I felt. She was furious when I finally came clean and told her flat out there was no way I was skiing with them that weekend.

"Because of a dream?" she'd exploded there in the hall, after listening to me so apparently patiently. "Because of a stupid dream you aren't going? How lame is that! C'mon," she pleaded. "C'mon, James, this is ridiculous!" She touched my arm. "Rooster? Please?"

She only called me by my nickname when she was trying to smooth things over between us, or ask a favour and that day at school, I just shook my head.

"Not gonna work," I said.

Frank at that point had mysteriously disappeared, and Jen and I were wedged in a crowd at the lockers between classes. She stamped her feet farther apart and leaned in at me, her books at a haphazard tilt in her arms.

"You cannot even think that I'd go without you! James? How can you think that? So this means that because you had a nightmare then none of us go? This means that one person can wreck everything for two other people? This means that all our plans are totally screwed? How fair is that? Would you want us to do this to you? Would you? How would you feel if we did this to you?"

Jen's on the debating team, and even though she's trained to not end every sentence in a question, she still does it when she's angry. And she was plenty angry. We'd been planning this trip, the three of us, for weeks, ever since Christmas break, and I knew she and Frank had both bought food and fought their parents for a chance to do this thing, but there was just no way I was going anywhere. I absolutely could not force myself to go this weekend. And I absolutely could not even begin to explain why to anybody. They had to just trust me.

"Look," I said reasonably, "there's no reason why you and Frank can't still go. He's a good guy; you know that. Nothing's gonna happen. You're safe with him."

"I'm not scared of being alone with Frankie," she practically spit at me. "I'm pissed, I am royally pissed, that you aren't coming along. You're the guy that started this whole thing." She glared at me, her eyes narrow, brows drawn down in a vee.

"Quitter," she said quietly. "Shirker." She has a very good vocabulary, thanks again to her time spent on the debating team. "Slacker."

Theoretically, she could have gone on calling me names for quite a while, but I cut in.

"I'm sorry," I said, and I meant it. "I was really looking forward to this, but I can't go. I just can't go. Something's telling me not to go. It won't let me."

That weird chick who seems to constantly crop up in the worst times pushed past me to get at her locker.

"Hey Ari," I mumbled and moved back before she actually stepped on me. She had shoved her way between Jen and me and, true to form, hadn't even seemed to notice. She was obviously struggling to remember her combination, living as she does in some crazy world of her own.

"Look," I continued, trying to talk past her, to reach Jen, whose dark brown eyes were narrowed with anger, "maybe you shouldn't go either. Maybe you guys should just stay home. We could do something else. A movie. Something."

Her mouth drooped, and you could almost see the steam coming out of her. "Not all of us are defeatist, negative, stupid laggards! What do you mean 'something's telling you not to go?' What 'something?' How can you talk like that?"

This was the point when Ari turned around and struggled through between us again. "Sorry!" she cried. "Sorry! Don't mind me." She looked at me, head cocked to one side. "Oh," she said and then reached out a hand and patted the air around my shoulder. "Hmmm," she said. "Well, gotta go!" And she was off.

Jen widened her eyes in disbelief at Ari's disappearing back, her anger forgotten for a brief second.

"She is such a freak," she stated, her normal response when Ari appears, and then turned back to me and got right back on topic again.

"So, let me understand this." She ticked the points off on her fingertips. "You are staying home and Frank and me are heading to the mountains. We bought a bunch of food, but you don't care." She paused for emphasis, and then ticked off another finger. "We planned this thing for two solid months and you just don't care! I practically had to fall on my *knees* to get my parents to agree and once again, you just don't freakin' care! Fine. Just great. Remember this next week when we have a fantastic time out there, skiing and hanging out, and we come back and you are out of the loop, buddy. Totally. Out. Of. The. *Loop*!"

"Just stay here," I coaxed. "Stay home. Call it off and we'll go another time."

"No." When she gets on an idea, Jen is determined, if nothing else. She's smart and she's cute with dark brown curly hair and a dancer's body, but she's also stubborn when she thinks she's right. Which is most of the time.

"No," she said. "Frank is a great guy. Really. He's really a nice guy. A super guy. He won't let me down." She turned the knife just a little bit more. "I used to have a huge crush on him a couple of years ago. I liked him 'way more than I liked you." Her eyes were narrowed as she gauged my reaction. "Do you even have any idea how hard it was to convince my parents of this? Do you? Any idea? No idea?"

It's kinder, I think, to simply tune her out when she gets this way. I've had lots of practice ignoring women by living all my life with mom, and so I switched Jen off and watched as Ari wandered past again, heading the wrong direction as usual, until she bumped into the one and only person in school who doesn't seem to mind how strange she is. Deena reached out and turned Ari around. I shook my head and tuned back in to Jen.

"Maybe Frankie and I will get something going on," she finished. She sounded triumphant. She was playing her last card, which was obvious. "Maybe he'll sweep me off my feet! Maybe you and I will be over after this. A romantic camping trip alone with Frank, in the dark, snowy mountains. Anything could happen."

"Yeah." The buzzer was gonna go any second, and I was getting tired of the conversation. "Might happen, I guess." I snaked out an arm and yanked her in to me, her books slamming on the floor. "But you'd miss me," I whispered in her ear. "You'd come back to me."

She grunted and hauled herself out of my arms, turning with a toss of her head, as she hunkered down to pick up her books. "Dreamer," she shot back at me as I left. "You're living a dream, James! You're not that hot! You're not that special!"

Which is the last thing she said to me that day, the thing that will probably ring in my head forever, because I didn't see her again for the rest of the afternoon. She was avoiding me—that much was obvious—and I was actually OK with it. There are worse things than being ignored, and one of those worse things is listening to somebody go on and on about something you've done that you can't change. Such as deciding not to go on a backwoods camping and cross-country ski trip with your two best friends.

Frank was more understanding, particularly since he now had the pleasure of hanging with Jen all weekend on his own, but even he was distant. I barely saw him all day, and he didn't catch the bus home after school. He left early to get his car gassed up and make sure they had all the camping gear packed.

And I went home alone. Just me and my hang-ups.

4

Two days later everything slammed to a solid halt. I'd spent most of Saturday hanging idly at home, watching the snow fall in giant wet flakes, sulking and morose and imagining in grim detail what I was missing. And missing only because of my inability to deal with the violent reality of that dream. What a loser. I was disgusted with myself, with my fears and my failures. What a lame wreck. I should have laughed that whole episode off, been a man, grown a pair and realized it was only some stupid dream out of my subconscious. I should be out for the weekend with my friends. My great friends who were probably having a fantastic time by themselves, without me. Crap.

By Sunday morning, I was a wreck. Tense and itchy like a fuse waiting for a light, I couldn't stop wondering what Jen and Frank were doing. Imagining them out there in the snow, making the tent all cozy and building a huge fire at night for fun, watching the stars come out together. I was wondering how cold it was up there in the mountains and what they might be doing in order to stay warm. Wondering if the skiing was as stupendous as I thought it would be, considering the snow that had fallen down here on the plains, wondering how deep the new snow was over the older packed stuff and imagining how fantastic smokies cooked over the fire must be tasting. I kicked myself over and over for letting my dream make me so freaky. And I was sorry as hell that I hadn't just ignored the dream's emotional fallout and gone with them.

I'd be a lot sorrier before I was finished, though, because around noon Frank's mom called, and although I remember answering the phone and saying hello to her, I have absolutely no recall of what happened after that, other than a cloud of words coming out of the speaker bringing with them an immensity of huge, black dread. A couple of minutes later mom caught a glimpse of my face and pulled the phone away from me. My knees were trembling and I nearly collapsed before she shoved me down onto a chair.

"What's wrong?" she demanded into the phone. "Who is this?"

My heart was thumping so hard I could barely hear, but the look dawning on her face was one of mute shock as Mrs. Bank's garbled story started to make sense to her. It was the same sort of expression I could feel growing on my own face. The horror of hearing that quiet, familiar voice speaking things nobody wanted to think about would stay with me all my life.

The police came by next, with both of Frank's parents huddled, silent and pale, in the rear seat of the squad car. Both wore expressions of stunned acceptance, as if a part of them had always been anticipating disaster of this sort.

What struck me then and still sticks with me now, is how busy everyone seemed to become—shaking hands and introducing themselves, taking off boots and coats, finding hangers, choosing places to sit. They were like human whirlwinds winding through our living room and into the dining room.

After hanging up jackets and greeting the cops, Mom took one long look at Frank's parents, yanked out a couple of chairs for them in the dining room, and immediately pulled me into the kitchen behind her.

"James," she said almost in a whisper, as she poured water into the coffee carafe, "give me a hand and get some of those things down for me, please."

'Things?' When I didn't move, she tried again. "James!" she hissed, "put those things on the table for me. Those things you drink from."

"Cups?" I asked, trying to keep my voice down so the cops and Frank's parents couldn't hear. Mom's behaviour is embarrassing a lot of the time and her actions often make me mad, but at that point my main focus was keeping her oddness under wraps. I didn't want her showing a couple of strange cops and Frank's parents how bizarre and weird she could sometimes be. What was happening here in our house was too important for her to wreck it with her crazy words and behaviour.

"Are you talking about cups?" I asked again, trying to keep my voice steady, trying to keep the building anger out of it.

Her eyes were blank when she stopped what she was doing, turned and gazed at me. "Those things you drink from!" she insisted. Her tone was frustrated now and rising with irritation. "You know! The things you put coffee in? What are they called?"

She slammed the flat of her hand on the sink. "Honestly," she said and tried a helpless short laugh. "My head these days! I just don't know where it's at sometimes."

"Cups, Mom. They're called 'cups.' I shook my head at her and then turned and pulled a few mugs out of the cupboard, placing them on a tray along with milk and sugar, trying to control my shaking hands.

To my relief she stopped talking after that, except for offering coffee and cookies. She made herself scarce in the kitchen, refilling the sugar bowl, making pot after pot of coffee and serving it to anyone who wanted it. It was uncharacteristic of her. Normally when things go down, she's loud and brazen, trying to bulldoze her way out of a tough situation by sheer willpower. That Sunday was different.

The police were polite but intense. There were two of them, and their radios kept buzzing and breaking into the conversation. One of them was older, and he sat back in his chair, his shoulders curved, stomach jutting out over his belt, writing stuff in a little notepad and sometimes listening in to his radio, evidently communicating with the RCMP up in Jasper. The other was younger, not very much older than me, with short blond hair and the beginnings of a beard shadow. He seemed tired. He leaned over the table, his bright blue eyes staring into my brown ones, practically willing the information out of me.

They wanted to know where we'd planned to go skiing. Exactly where. No estimating distances, or brushing it off with just saying south of Jasper on the Parkway. Not a chance of that. Where? Which cutline? Which little cabin off the highway? Which closed trail that all we had to do was lift the chain and we could drive right in to the summertime parking lot? Which?

"That's the place, all right. The car's been found," one of them was saying. "The car's there. It's the right car."

The older cop looked at me, then off into the distance. "Your friends left the chain off and someone else followed them in. Those people were the ones who called in the distress call. They saw the avalanche come down." He glanced at me again, his eyes remote. "There wasn't anything they could do."

My head was spinning. It was hard to know if I was standing in my real life or somehow parachuting into a different life, a different universe, where unseen dangers crept through cracks and attacked the people I loved. A place where giant birds actually did drop loads of frozen spearheaded feathers that choked and chilled and killed. My hands wouldn't stop trembling and my legs felt like those knotted ropes magicians use, where they stay stiff and then suddenly collapse in a weak heap.

And because they asked, I drew a little map for them with wavy lines indicating the highway, the parking lot that's open in summer for tourists who want to hike the trail up to Marion Lake, but closed in winter, with a chain across it. The trail that leads from that parking lot up into the high country and a little abandoned cabin up on what Frank and I call 'Rocky Ridge' because of the piles of tumbled rocks we'd discovered up there last July.

I sketched in the various places I figured the tent might have been pitched and I listened as they spoke about the other people, birdwatchers who'd seen a couple of people skiing way far up on the distant slope and then watched as a huge cloud of white came down, obliterating any sign of the skiers. The people who'd run back down to the parking lot and then, their cell signal not working that far along the Parkway, driven back to Jasper to report a possible catastrophe on Mount Hesker.

Through the entire conversation, I had a movie going on in my head of the day Frank and I hiked up the pathway last summer when the place was full of little wild orchids and other tiny flowers,

springing up out of the mossy ground cover. And the day we'd strag-
gled up again in early fall, not expecting anything except clear, crisp
fall weather and found instead, a crazy, wild snowstorm that bubbled
up over the cleft in the mountains to the west and dumped a few
inches of soft, dry powder on us.

We had been completely unprepared for snow that weekend, but
because it was still fall and relatively warm even at night, we man-
aged to simply put up with our damp socks and jeans and actually
race around in the stuff and have fun. It wasn't dangerous. It wasn't
intimidating or potentially lethal. It was white and soft. Pretty.

As the cops talked, Frank's parents sat quietly, sipping weak, luke-
warm coffee without complaint, while mom buzzed around them
offering cookies and filling their cups again and again. Both cops
kept their cups full. I sat.

My hands were resting weakly on my knees, my head seeming
to bob all over the place while I tried to answer questions, tried to
describe what I thought Frank and Jen would have been wearing,
where they would have tried to ski down Mount Hesker, why they
went up there in the first place, and a million other questions. They
finally all left, but not until the two cops made sure we had their numbers so we could call if I remembered anything else. Frank's parents
were quiet as they left the house, heads sunken between shoulders,
holding hands against what was bound to come.

And I went to my room. Mom stayed out in the dining room,
cleaning the table, washing up dishes, silent still and keeping herself
busy before knocking on my door and then leaving a supper plate
on the hall carpet outside my room. I couldn't face her. Didn't want
to see anyone.

Staying home from school on Monday wasn't an option, at least not
for me. Mom spent most of Sunday night and all of the next morning, before she left for work, trying to convince me to take what she
called a 'personal' day. Stay home. Get some rest. Yak-yak-yak. As
if staying home was going to solve anything, or bring anyone back.
I needed to get out of the house and away from that place where the
memory of cops sitting around the house and Frank's mom softly

crying at the dining table were echoing around in my head like a howling pack of mourning dogs.

And a part of me didn't actually believe Frank and Jen were officially missing. A part of me expected to see him at the bus stop, running late, looking goofy. Or mad at me still for not going with them. Either way. Didn't matter. Just so long as he was there, which of course, he wasn't. But I needed to see they weren't there. I needed to look for them in the halls by their lockers, and realize that Frank wasn't at his normal table during Chem or hanging out backstage during Drama watching girls.

It was in the middle of my crafts class that some of the reality began to strike home. Ignoring the commiserating looks from teachers and other kids, I was trying to get another project completed for marking. Earlier in the year I'd decided working with stained glass was my best option in the Fine Arts section of the curriculum, since I'd never been able to actually draw or paint or even sketch. Stained glass meant drawing out a rough concept called a 'cartoon,' then making sure all the joining lines were actually workable with the glass and solder, then tracing and refining the drawing until it looked good. It was soothing to cut the glass, grind it down and then fit it all together like a puzzle.

I'd built a suncatcher for Jen at Christmas—a lopsided pink heart with a lot of coloured glass beads surrounding it and dripping down from the bottom point. She'd cried when she unwrapped the thing. It hung in the window of her bedroom, and she told me once that she looked at it first thing every morning and last thing every night. Of course, she wasn't mad at me when she told me that. Could be that while she grabbed her stuff to head out of town with Frank, she not only didn't look at it, maybe she even took it down or decided she hated it.

And yet, even while I stood there alone at my workstation, moving the various pieces of glass around on the light table, searching out the best combinations of colour and density, a part of me still expected Frank to jump around the corner and offer a bag of chips or a soda. Smack me in the arm or drag me into a headlock and send the glass stuff flying.

Part of me still expected to have Jen show up and start bawling me out for dropping the ball and missing the trip. Insisting I meet all kinds of wild demands proving my guilt and shame and offering a chance for penance for ever having disappointed her in the first place. Forcing me to co-operate with whatever crazy activity she came up with for me to make it up to her and show how sorry I was. She had a battering-ram way of proving her point through overwhelming any opposition by single-minded insistence in the belief that her view on any subject was totally right and mine totally wrong. It was difficult to argue with her absolute faith in her own opinions, particularly when those opinions revolved around how simple it could be for me to improve as her boyfriend.

A little piece inside my head was waiting for them both to be suddenly standing next to me in full cry, loud and impatient, teasing and jabbing at me for being a coward and staying home. And when none of that happened, all that was left was the empty echoing reality that nothing would ever be the same again.

5

Their bodies were found separately three days later, buried under several feet of snow. The avalanche had overtaken Jen first, catching her higher up the mountain, tumbling her down and leaving her in a small gully wedged against a broken tree trunk, a few metres behind Frank. He was in the open, away from the treeline, buried under a massive slab of semi-solid snowpack. It had caught them so quickly, neither had a chance to outrun the devastation. It probably happened too fast for each to yell a warning at the other. It's hard to know if they realized, even at the last minute, in those final seconds of life, what kind of devastation was upon them.

Frank had been in front, probably breaking trail. Frank loved the speed of skiing. Downhill was where he really shone, tearing through fresh snow, leaping moguls, bouncing down the straightest possible path and dodging slower skiers, but he loved the quiet and solitude of cross-country too. He wouldn't have wanted to be behind Jen, slowed down by her. Jen was always more cautious whenever she did anything athletic, and I knew she'd have been skiing more carefully than Frank, easing her way down the slope.

Jen's talent, the thing that had drawn her to the arts school program, was violin. Music was what made her life rich, and she was aiming at a career playing with the Edmonton Symphony, so she worried about bruises and bumps on her arms and hands. I'd loved the look of her arms, strong and tensed, when she held her bow before taking off on some crazy wild riff. In my mind I could see her skiing cautiously, taking the turns long and slow with wide uphill swoops, slowing herself for the downward arcs.

The rescue dogs found her. A golden retriever named Daisy caught the trail and dug down to where one hand, still wearing its glove, stuck out away from her body, reaching towards the surface. The gloves she wore were bright blue with blinding-white snow-flakes knitted into their backs. There was no way of mistaking them.

Her poor hand. It was the only mental picture I could get my head around. Everything else was simply too rough to deal with. An arm, a hand with a glove on it. Picturing their battered bodies was impossible.

In the turmoil of the avalanche she'd lost her skis. They were found scattered and broken, several metres away from where she lay. She and Frank had been above the treeline when the avalanche hit, probably anticipating a long, sloping run down the mountainside to where they'd camped in a grove of pine and poplar, and then after lunch, another hike up and another swooping glide down before set-tling in to get warm for the night and to rest up for skiing the next day.

The campsite was as they'd left it—a kettle for tea resting in the ashes of the fire and some kindling stacked near where they'd built their little fire for heat and cooking. The tent still stood with their stuff still inside, protected by the trees surrounding it, and off to the side of where the avalanche finally tumbled to a stop. The RCMP had taken lots of pictures of the site and the places where Frank and Jen were found. Because it was my tent they'd been using, I had to identify it and some of the other gear.

The tent, a little two-man one I'd found in a garage sale when I was a kid and bugged mom about for hours before she gave in and went down to talk to the guy, wasn't even torn. It was wrinkled from being packed up for the trip, but otherwise perfectly okay when I picked it up from the station after identifying for them what was left from the camping trip. It seemed there should have been visible dam-age. Slashes, gashes, broken branches sticking out of it, something to prove it had survived such horror—a broken zipper, even, but there was nothing to mark the disaster. Just the bright blue and yellow of a dome tent Frank and I had used since our early days camping in each other's backyards.

Afterward, there were stories in the paper for a couple of days about two young people dying with their whole lives in front of them and what a waste it all had been. There were responding letters to the editor about how stupid it is for people to go off-trail and into the backcountry, risking their lives for the sake of adventure and the thrill of being alone in virgin snow. Questions were asked about whether or not public money should be spent on private searches that put the searchers themselves at physical risk.

I wanted to smash these people who wrote the letters—knock their heads in for asking their questions, offering their unwanted and useless opinions, for their still being alive on this planet. None of it mattered. Jen was dead. Frank was dead.

And I was alive. Alive and struggling to come to some sort of understanding with it all. A truce. I needed a truce for the battle raging in my own head where it seemed maybe I could have warned them somehow. Maybe if I'd tried harder to convince them to stay home they'd still be alive and breathing. Even thinking that, I knew they'd never have listened to me. They'd have laughed and joked and gotten mad at me, and then they'd have gone on the trip anyway.

The realization infuriated me. My anger was so deep and so dark I could barely even look at mom when she tried to draw me out, tried to make me talk and share. Part of me just wanted to yell and keep on yelling and never stop. There was a mental picture in my head of a man on his knees, with his head thrown back in a scream of rage, arms stiff at his sides, fists clenched, helpless. And it was me.

What really scared me was the thought maybe the dream had caused this to happen. Maybe my having that dream was a catalyst of some sort, changing the tilt of the world and sending the whole black episode into existence. Whenever my head started running in this direction, I had no choice but to make it stop. I couldn't go there. Not yet. In no way was I ready to examine the dream, the bird, the chilling experience of choking on the silvery sharp flakes dropping out of a dark, careless sky.

At the same time it obsessed me—the dream itself and the desire to examine it, countered with the opposing inability to relive it. I couldn't let it go. I wasn't eating. I wasn't sleeping. The only things keeping me upright and moving through each day were rage and fantasies of somehow getting revenge. Avenging their deaths through making someone else, or something else, suffer like they'd suffered. Like I was suffering. Some days I felt like I was sleepwalking my way through life, like all the other people were aliens of some sort who had nothing to do with me. Other days I was more alive than I'd ever been, filled as I was with a boiling pot of rage, revenge and venom. Until it all got to the point where others began taking notice.

"James," Mom started one night, "come here and talk to me."

She was sitting on the sofa with the remote in her lap, the TV muted, and a drink in her hand. She rattled the ice cubes in her glass and took a sip of rye and seven, then patted the cushion next to her.

"C'mon," she urged. "You'll feel better. Really. You will."

"No." I leaned on the door frame and shook my head. "No, I won't feel better."

There was something too awful in the thought Mom assumed I could be soothed like a kid who'd stubbed his toe. Soothed into not thinking the awful thoughts that filled my head. Soothed just because she wanted the tension in the house to ease up, so her life would be better.

"This is not your choice, Mom," I said. "This is my choice how I handle this. You barely even knew them."

"What? How can you say that?" Her voice rose with indignation. She stared over at me with a sort of unfocused intensity, as if she couldn't see me very well. "I've known Frankie Banks since he was a little boy. I used to have coffee with his mom all the time."

" 'All the time!'" I knew it was wrong to take my frustration out on her, but I did it anyway. "You barely knew her. You were so busy dating every guy you could get your hands on all you did was drop me off at their place and take off on your own. You never had coffee with her. You never stuck around. I bet you hardly remembered her name when she showed up at the door that day."

"James! I resent that." She tipped her glass back again and turned her eyes to the pictures filling the tube. She had the TV tuned into some ridiculous reality show. The kind of 'reality' that is miles away from being real in any normal person's universe.

"Frank's mom and I were good friends for quite a while," she said, her eyes still looking at the screen, away from me, "even though we didn't see very much of each other lately. It's just that you enjoyed being there so much and they had that dog you loved to play with. And Frank had a lot more toys because his parents had a lot more money.

"Don't forget"—her tone turned into lecture mode—"that I had to struggle all by myself to support the two of us. Don't forget that."

"Yeah, I know." I'd heard it all before and truthfully, it was ultimately kind of boring.

"Come on," she pleaded. "Come sit with your old Mom and tell her what's on your mind. Tell me what's bugging you."

What's bugging me? The phrase was so out of whack with what had happened, it left me speechless for a second. I sagged away from the frame and the TV and her and started to turn away.

"Nothing's 'bugging' me, Mom. I'm fine." I was leaving the room and she suddenly reared up in her seat.

"Don't you dare walk out on me!" she yelled. "Don't you dare ignore me like you always do! I'm trying to help. I'm trying to be your mom and help you!"

Drinks and dramatics. Happens a lot around my place, and it's one reason she didn't really know Frank all that well and had only met Jen at school functions. I kept my personal life personal, meaning that she was in one little box in my life and my friends and the other people I loved or liked or hated were in another box. Keeping her under the radar and located where I could control her was important.

"Mom, I'm gonna go listen to music," I said. "I'll be in my room."

"Why can't you be easier!" she screamed. Her drink splashed onto her blouse and she dabbed at the droplets with her free hand. "Why is everything always so hard with you?"

It was finally more than I could stand. I've lived with these outbursts all my life and mostly I've learned to ignore them, tiptoe around them and let them go. Not this time, though.

"My best friend died, Mom! He died! Don't you get that?"

"Ohhh." The word was a long, drawn-out sob. "Oh, James," she said, tears hovering, "you'll make other friends, James. You will." And then her tone hardened again and she sniffled the tears back. "I'm your friend, James. Me. I can be your best friend."

It was too pathetic. Somehow her words had gone beyond being shameful and useless and had become more than anything damaging. Damaging to her, to me and to our weak-kneed mother-son relationship.

"How can you not get this?" Disgust and disappointment welled up inside, choking me. The blood was pounding in my head and my voice, when it came out again, sounded thick even to my own ears. "How can you not understand? What do you expect from me, Mom?"

"I expect . . ." She dwindled off and sobbed for a moment. Then she took a swig from what remained in her glass and started in on me again. "I expect you to treat me with respect."

"I do, Mom. I do treat you with respect." It took all my strength to stand there and continue the conversation. It was impossible to know how much of what she said came from the drink in her hand and how much from in her heart. And I wasn't sure if this was her first drink or her third. Who knew? She might be sober or she might be well on her way to passing out.

"I do respect you, Mom," I said more softly. "Honest. I just want to listen to some music. OK?"

"Sit down and watch some TV instead," she said, sounding tired now. "Just sit with me for a while. Please?"

"Mom, I can't. I'll be just down the hall, though. I won't go anywhere."

I edged out of the room and she sagged back onto the sofa and turned up the sound on her program.

6

For the first week after they were found I was consumed with an inconsolable fury; all my energy came from there, and in my anger I did everything I could to erase the bald fact of their deaths and live what I thought should be a normal life.

I shoved my feelings deep down inside and kept up the routine. I went to school, shovelled the sidewalks, tried to stop Mom from drinking too much at night and made sure my grades didn't slide. I talked past the sodden looks of commiseration from teachers and friends, their crying eyes and efforts to hug me, in an attempt to keep our conversations on an ordinary track of school and weather. I was not into talking about my feelings with anyone or having anybody see me break down and cry. As if crying would ever solve or absolve anything. It wasn't until the end of that week, after the memorial services, I crashed. Crashed and burned for a while.

The fury I felt at how they'd both gone and died on me consumed me, and it was getting harder and harder to hide myself from it, but at the same time I still wasn't interested in talking to anyone about any of it. Who was ever gonna understand? Who was ever gonna see how guilty I was in all this, how reprehensible it was that I'd stayed safe and warm at home, how wrong I'd been to be so scared, how I'd ultimately let down my two best friends and however inadvertently been the cause of their death, their anguish and fear before they'd died. The fear they must have felt as they got swallowed by the mad, crashing snow was why I could never forgive myself.

The anger boiling inside was the only thing that made me certain I was still alive, and I wanted only to wallow around in raging recriminations against them and me. How could they have been so stupid? Maybe if they'd been less bullheaded and had listened to me they'd be alive now. And then the thoughts would go further and I'd find myself thinking that if I'd been more open about the strength of the dream they might have believed me. If I hadn't been so afraid of being laughed at for the bird thing, and the feeling of smothering under those icy feathers, maybe they'd have stayed home. If that was the case, then it was my fault they died. And that's when the anger took over again, because following those thoughts to their logical conclusion was unbearable.

At home there was nothing to distract me from all the loathing burning inside, and it got so I hated being there, hated having to walk in the door every afternoon and look at the empty rooms, waiting for Mom to come home. At least at school I had to walk the halls, appear in classes, open my locker and look inside.

"Hey." I was in the shop at school, absently moving glass pieces around the cartoon pattern I'd been working on, lost in the circling demons of blame and denial, anger and fear. "Can you make me something for real cheap?"

Ari stood next to my worktable, her hands clasped in front of her as if anticipating my answer would be a negative one and she'd need to plead. Her long neck supported a head covered in hair cut so short it resembled dandelion fuzz more than actual human hair. Her head looked wobbly on its neck, like a too-large flower bud on a skinny stem.

"What?" I asked stupidly. She was the first person who'd talked to me in a normal voice all week. It threw me.

"Something cheap," she replied, emphasizing the 'cheap.' "Because as usual I have no money and as usual I have to figure out something to give somebody that isn't going to actually cost me money that I don't have. We could barter," she ended brightly.

"Barter?"

"Trade. I could give you something in return. Although, it's kinda hard to think of anything you might want that I could actually give. Would you maybe want an origami thingy, which my dad makes by the dozens, so I could get you lots? As many as you want, really. Y'know, like birds and flowers and stuff? He's an origami wizard. Sort of. If there is such a thing. Totally into koalas at the moment."

She paused, and before I could say anything, jumped in again. "He gets a lot of paper cuts. Lots. Some of them are really deep. He loves, loves, loves origami. Says it's meditative. So, do you want to trade for some of it?"

At my look, she shook her head and continued. "Yeah. No. I didn't think so. How did those barter systems even work back in the old days or in those countries where they still do that stuff?" She stopped for a second and then said brightly, "Do you like bread? Because I do know how to bake bread. I make really awesome bread. And of course the ingredients are free because they're in the bottom cabinet and Mom never has a clue and so I could bake extra bread and give you a loaf. Would that be OK?"

"Bread?"

I was standing there, my mouth drooping open in an attempt to follow her train of thought as it wandered seemingly at random all over the place. "Yeah, I guess I like bread."

"Great! Bread it is!" She grinned up at me and then hoisted herself up onto a stool and crossed her legs as if settling in for a while. "Bread's good. I like it, too. Especially hot and fresh. Really awesome."

Ari broke off and examined a fingernail and, figuring she was done talking, I bent down again over my cartoon where it was spread out on the worktable.

"Hey, so Deena's aunt's birthday is in two weeks," she said, "so I need it for then. She's the one that taught me to make bread. She makes everything: brown bread, fry bread, these awesome little buttery rolls, muffins. Cinnamon buns! And it's all really easy and really good so you'll honestly love this stuff.

"So"—she paused for a breath, and if I'd been thinking straight I'd have jumped in there and got her stopped—"can you make me something for then? She's a really neat lady. Doesn't have to be big or anything. Could be just something small. Maybe a wolf or something? She likes wolves and coyotes. She remembers them howling sometimes when she lived up north. When she was little. Must've been kind of wild and scary, but she says it was honestly really haunting and cool. She hasn't actually lived up north for a long time, but I thought maybe a wolf to remind her of her childhood. But then I wasn't even sure if you could do a wolf in stained glass. Would it look like a wolf? She could hang it in her window. In the kitchen."

It was starting to look like this could go on indefinitely.

"Fine." I broke in, not rudely exactly, but intending to leave no doubt in her head that the conversation was officially finished. "I'll do it. You can have it next week."

"Really?" The thrill in her voice was so apparent it practically split my skull, which had been aching for days now. "That's freakin' awesome! Thank you!"

"Yeah, whatever. Fine." I waited for her to leave.

She continued to sit there on the stool, a huge grin pasted on her face, her dandelion head bobbing around as if she was keeping time to some music playing somewhere that only she could hear.

"Well?" I didn't even bother to keep the sarcasm from my voice. "Is there anything else?"

"Nope. Not now." She hopped down from the stool. "I can see them around you, y'know. And not just them. Others, too. See ya." And she left.

Jen had been right, I thought dully; she's just plain weird. And at the memory of Jen, I slumped down on the stool Ari'd been perched on and let my head sag down between my shoulders, lost and completely alone.

7

The entire school was officially invited to the joint memorial service for Frank and Jen, but not very many people actually came. The teachers were there of course, along with the younger cop from that first Sunday when Frank and Jen were still only missing, and some of the people we'd all hung out with, but a lot of other people just didn't show and I didn't entirely blame them. The weather was awful, for one thing. Amazingly cold. Minus 35 with the wind chill, and hard pellets of snow blowing all over the roads. It was so cold the moisture inside my nose froze, making me want to rub my nose and bend it to break the ice forming inside. Typical weather for springtime in Alberta.

Technically speaking, early March isn't exactly spring, but in mid-February before the skiing weekend, the weather had turned warmer and some of the optimists among us were anticipating an early spring. This weekend, which now forever would be the memorial weekend for me, was a return to reality. Winter in Alberta isn't over until it says it's over. The streets were skating rinks. The cold and the frost had hardened the road surface until it became black, skiddery ice, so probably a lot of people decided to do their own grieving at home where it was warm.

It didn't matter, anyway. The memorial was just one more thing to get through. Sitting there in a room at the funeral joint, it was like being in a weird practical joke or another offbeat dream. It couldn't be real. The caskets were up there at the front. Jen's casket was covered in flowers. Frank's had pictures—one of him at 10 on a bike, another of him wearing a crazy, vee-shaped grin.

There was a seemingly endless round of heartbreaking eulogies and teary-eyed musical numbers, and my mind wandered away into memories from the past, bringing up mental pictures of Frankie when we were both little, before we knew anything bad could ever happen to us. When we were invincible . . .

"That's just the cat's ass, man! Too cool!"

Frankie held a magazine he'd scammed from one of the bigger kids in school, probably the one kid in Grade Six who was always grubby and picking fights at random with kids older than him and who had probably swiped the thing from his dad. The magazine was full of crazy-looking cars and women hanging around, draped over bumpers, wearing skimpy bathing suits, big hair and wide smiles. Frank was about seven, his cheeks were wind-chapped and red and his eyes glittering at saying what he thought of as a 'bad' word. Taboo. 'Ass' could get you in all kinds of trouble.

The memory of Frank back about 10 years ago ran like a thin thread through my head. A corner of my mouth turned up; I couldn't help it. His made up his own nickname: 'Fearless Frank.' He called me 'Senor Chickenman'. We were just little kids who thought we were tough guys. He was always such a funny dude, even when he was really little. We'd been such goofy kids together. Boys who were obsessed by weird body noises and disgusting smells. Farting. Farting broke us up every time. We liked our bikes, our Frisbees, his dog and basically anything other people thought was inappropriate. We laughed like wild things and we built spaceships and time capsules out of old cardboard boxes.

And then again, another memory of Frank popped up, this one from only a couple of years ago, returning to the subject of cats again.

"Hey, man," he'd said, "watch this." And he'd pursed his lips. "Like a cat's ass, right?"

"'Cat's ass'? What?" I remembered he'd given me a knuckle-smack hard in the arm for not following his train of thought.

It was a miracle, I thought there at the memorial, that I even had arms anymore after all the abuse they'd been through. Frank's biggest thrill had been to knock me in the arm, most of the time just for fun, but sometimes in pure anger.

"You know," he'd insisted that day, making an exaggerated kissy face, his lips pursed tight, "like this." He could barely talk. "Just like a cat's rear end, man."

"You're disgusting." I remembered myself laughing like a crazy man. He was just so unpredictably funny. "You're an idiot."

"No, seriously. A cat's butt is a perfect little," and again he pursed his lips, "like a rose, y'know, a little rose." He rolled his eyes wildly to add to the effect. "A perfect specimen of a little pink rose. That's me. She's gonna love me, man! Once she gets to know the real me." He socked me in the arm again, and I plowed him back.

During his most recent cat's-ass phase, Frank had been talking for weeks about wanting to ask some girl out. He'd been pursuing her with single-minded zeal, but she'd become pretty skilled at avoiding him. He was thinking pink roses would change her mind. In his mind, of course, pink roses had then somehow morphed into cat's behinds. He'd found it tough to locate girls who shared his sense of humour. For obvious reasons.

They were up there by the caskets, talking through tears of the talents, the gifts, the heart-destroying loss, and I was sitting there with the rest of the mourners, a half-grin pasted on my face.

It was completely against all protocol, it was completely inappropriate and also ultimately embarrassing, but when I got up finally to make what I hoped would be a dry-eyed, roughly 30-second speech in memory of both Jen and Frank, what I ended up doing was laughing through my tears while I described Frank's first attempts at throwing a Frisbee when he was about five years old. He threw it hard and fast and then forgot to let go of the thing and ended by hitting himself hard in the head. He had a bump over his eye for a week, which once he'd stopped crying over, he'd started bragging about. Told everyone he'd had to defend me from vicious Viking raiders. The horn on one guy's hat had smacked him in the eye and he'd taken quite a beating before he got the better of the other guys.

And I talked about the time in Grade Three when Frank decided the upcoming Family Dance was the perfect opportunity to put the moves on Chantelle, a black-haired little girl two grades higher, whom he thought was the most beautiful girl alive. Frank always aimed high. Problem was, he wasn't sure if the night would play out according to his high hopes, and just for the sake of safety, he decided he needed to practise his masculine technique.

Kissing was foreign territory for both of us, except for our moms and his grandma. To his credit, he realized even at that young age, it was not the kind of kissing that would get him anywhere with an older woman like Chantelle. Frank had a favourite truck at the time, however —a red and yellow plastic dump truck complete with working gears and a little shovel. He took the thing out of his backyard and into the tub, washed it with his mom's kiwi shampoo to give it what he called a 'nice smell,' and named it "Sherry" after his grandma's favourite after-dinner drink. He then practised his kissing on the front bumper. Which I had to admit at the time, did have a striking resemblance to the lips of the actual girl of his dreams.

And then I described Jen's fumbling attempts at teaching me to behave like a proper boyfriend. The massive talking-and-sharing marathons, conducted eye to eye, emptying our hearts to each other with a seriousness that bordered on international diplomatic relations and that usually ended with her leaning back, looking satisfied, and me sitting there lost in a fog of confusion. I detailed some of our long negotiations regarding the impact of hand-holding at school and the extremely touchy subject of who pays for what, when my finances were stretched to the limit by movie and pizza demands. I shared her tactics used in changing me for the better, which included bribery, threats of physical harm and blackmail.

By the time I was finished it felt like I'd been up there for hours, but in reality it was 10 minutes, and people were laughing while they wiped their eyes.

8

That night Frank came and sat on my chest. He was heavy. It was the middle of the night and I was sleeping soundly until the moment when a weighty thing settled down on me and made it impossible to breathe. The suffocating weight of it woke me out of a dreamless sleep.

There was nothing and nobody there, of course, as I woke in the dark, but I could still feel that heavy thing crushing my chest. Frank and I had always wrestled, especially when we were kids, and I was familiar with the gasping panic of being unable to suck in air while he sank his entire body weight on my ribs. Frank's favourite move was to snake a long skinny leg behind one of mine, forcing my knee to bend and flipping me down before sitting on my chest with his knees pressed into my ribcage. For such a skinny guy he was really strong. His knobby bones had hurt like hell where they cut into me.

Mostly we wrestled for fun, for something to do, something to take the itch away, but sometimes it could get pretty serious, and I still remembered one time when he was furious about some forgotten thing I'd said or done. He sat there with his knees pressed into my ribcage, my hands trapped under my body so I was completely helpless. He was cocky, sitting upright with his knees pressed into me, my hands pinned under my butt, poking at me with his long skinny fingers, stabbing me in the eyes and ears and laughing his head off. We were just kids, hanging in his bedroom, and we'd been horsing around with some of his stuff, but somehow things went sideways. It was so bad I hoped his mom would hear us and come to break things up.

Trying to dislodge him through twisting my body and kicking out with my legs had only led to frustration for me and triumph for him. Nothing worked and it was getting so I thought my ribs were gonna break. I could barely breathe and in my desperation to get free, I'd wound up a huge gob of spit.

"Yeah," he'd said, staring down at me, his blue eyes little pinpoints of anger. "Try it. Just try it."

And I'd thought better of the plan and swallowed the gob back down.

"Let me up, man," I'd said, my voice hoarse and rasping in my ears, my head pounding with the tempo of blood pumping through it.

We were only about 10 years old, and it took a lot to get him pissed at me, but Frankie was one mean fighter when he was mad. It hurt so bad and I was so embarrassed and mad that I was nearly in tears, which in turn made me even angrier. I'd twisted my hips, trying to throw him off, and one hip was turned sideways with the leg splayed out at a painful angle.

"Get off!" I coughed out, and finally he rose slowly, his hands raised in a phoney show of peace and goodwill, a smirk on his freckled mug.

My immediate reaction was to smack him down, but catching my breath was more important and I stood there, swallowing my tears, rubbing my ribs and hoping he'd die in some terrible way. Maybe get eaten alive by a crocodile, or run over by a lady driver, which would be completely humiliating as well as making him dead and making me glad, or maybe getting stung by a little spider that would have crawled into his ear and bitten him in the brain. I was 10. Nothing was impossible.

Now I said it aloud again in the darkness of my room. "Get off me, man!"

And as I spoke the words the weight lifted. I could breathe again.

And I found myself staring into the dark void of my bedroom, its shadows lit only by the streetlight shining outside, and wondering what the hell had just happened.

9

"You probably don't even realize it, but you've opened a door,"
Ari said the next day. I'd made the mistake of telling her I was having some bizarre dreams. She was the first person I'd confided in
since the frustrating episode of telling mom about the bird dream.
"And believe me, you're gonna regret it, because it can really get to
be a pain."

She was chewing on a long strand of red liquorice, sitting on the
stool next to my workbench while I started tracing, on a brittle chunk
of brown swirling glass, the cartoon segments that would eventually
make up the wolf's body. The glass sheet was crazy hard to work
with. It was beautiful, with thin threads of swirling white and grey
cutting through depths of deep chocolate brown, but it was a piece
of old glass, thickened by the layers of colour, brittle and uneven,
and tracing on it was difficult. Cutting and grinding were going to
take a lot more time and care than usual.

"I come from probably the weirdest family on the planet," she
continued, seeming to not care that I was only half-listening, "and
it's something I'm pretty much an expert on. Opening doors, I mean.
They open and they shut, or they sit there just a little ajar, just teasing you. Doors and cracks in the universe. Just so weird. And not
something to mess around with, either, let me tell you!"

She was chewing on her candy, sitting there cross-legged, bal-
anced precariously as she continued. "And I didn't used to see them
around you before, but I see them around you now, so that's how I
know you've opened some kind of door."

I was definitely sorry I'd ever mentioned anything to her. I had zero idea what she was talking about and what she was seeing around me other than possibly simmering resentment at everyone else in the world who had their lives unravelling in a normal way instead of ending under tons of snow.

Truthfully, I had no idea why I'd confided in her in the first place, since she was not the type of girl I'm drawn to. She's odd in just about every way imaginable, including physically. I like my girls to be pretty, the kind other guys give a second look to, the kind who make me look good just by hanging around with me. Ari's skinny and she doesn't have much of a figure. Her clothes are almost unbelievably strange, like stuff you might pick up at a garage sale or second-hand store. One memorable morning she showed up at school wearing a red and yellow plaid lumberjack shirt over a faded Beatles tee, with cargo shorts, bright orange tights and black high-tops, and it was nowhere near Halloween. Believe me when I say her clothing choices normally do nothing for her in any way, except make her more of an outcast than she usually is.

Ari never wears makeup and she's usually got her nose shoved in a book. Her hair is cut so short she resembles a recovering cancer patient and her behaviour is consistently off the wall, as if she either doesn't know or doesn't care how odd she seems to other people. She can be kind of feisty, the sort of person who's not scared of what others think and argues a point no matter how much everyone else just wants the conversation to be over. She's got weird eyes. They're really the only memorable thing about her. Light blue, piercing, surrounded by a dark blue ring around the rim of the iris. Crazy eyes. They can feel like darts when she's pissed.

Her only friend in school seems to be Deena, another oddball who keeps to herself, but who, judging by her skin colour and her hair, is probably Metis like me. Not that it matters. It doesn't, at least not to me.

"Look." I was being uncharacteristically patient with her because it was so obvious she wasn't playing with a full deck. "Just leave me alone, OK? If you want this thing done, you've gotta let me work at it."

"Yeah," she nodded. And pulled another string of liquorice out of the bag. And scratched her ear and kept sitting there. Belatedly, she held the bag out to me, offering me a piece.

"But still," she continued, "it's fun to watch you do this stuff and, plus, Deena's rehearsing a play she wrote, which is all personal and stuff, and "—she waved her hands in the air—"she says I'm a distraction and she told me to go away, and I have nobody else to talk to."

"Right." I bent over the glass and traced carefully around a section of leg. "So you've gotta torment somebody and I'm the lucky one."

It suddenly struck me as suspicious. It wasn't like I was in the market for new friends or a girlfriend or anything like that. In fact, it was the opposite. I was intent on pulling into myself, hovering and nursing the solitude and the hurt. Talking to nobody.

"Why are you hanging around all the time? Don't you have anything else to do?"

She looked at me strangely. "You know, I've been asked that before," she said slowly. "Bizarre, huh?"

Not that bizarre.

"And honestly, I can honestly, honestly state that I have no freakin' clue. I don't know why I do what I do, and I don't even want to know. There's already way too much to think about."

"Uh-huh. Get lost."

"Seriously?"

"Seriously." I stood there with the glass cutter in hand and motioned at the door. Her time was up, and not just because I wanted to be alone again.

"When I start cutting, the glass splinters and little shards of glass start flying. Believe me when I say they hurt. You'd need to wear shop glasses if you want to hang out here, but they can still hit you in the face and get in your hair. They're nearly invisible, they stick in your skin and they're painful. So scram."

"OK." She hoisted herself down again and started for the door. "But don't forget, if you want to talk ever"—she was walking backward out of the workshop—"you can just call me. Or you know, get me online or something. I betcha I can help."

"Yeah. Look," I said, and maybe it was a little strong. "I don't want you hanging around. OK? Understand? I will do this thing for you, because you asked. But, I want to be by myself. I don't want company. Got it?"

"Got it." And she was gone.

And I was left staring at a piece of inanimate glass and a cartoon on the light table of a lone wolf in profile, howling against a full moon.

10

It was just another ordinary day in a string of ordinary days. Weeks had passed almost without my noticing it. I got up in time for school and went to bed at night, and every morning when I opened my eyes a bottomless void of loss and loneliness yawned in front of me. The world was dark and oppressive, populated by shadows of people—grey beings without faces or smiles, lacking any sense of light or hope. I moved through air that was thick and stifling. The bus ride to school, the classes at school, the kids in the hall—all of it was muffled, like someone had put a silencer on the days, and all that reached me through the density was a distant hum.

What I didn't see until much later was how this particular day marked a beginning. And an end. It marked a time when I was going to have to make a choice between options, none of which seemed like good ones at the time.

Like a car running down a deeply rutted road, the morning started like every other one lately, with memories and recriminations racing around in circles in my skull until I was dizzy with the effort of trying to follow them. I couldn't seem to twist the wheel hard enough to get my head to travel straight. Every time I thought I had the demons beat, the wheels of my thoughts would slide right back into the ruts and I'd be bouncing down a rough road again. Why them? Why not me? Why'd that dream happen? Was there something I was supposed to do with the dream that I didn't do, that I wasn't doing? Did the dream cause Jen and Frank to die? If I hadn't dreamed it, would they still be alive?

"Deena and I are heading to her place after school, wanna come?"

Ari's company had become a persistent presence in my life almost without my realizing it. After taking possession of the stained glass wolf, which I'd had to admit turned out pretty cool, with the profiled brown-swirling wolf howling in front of a yellow moon, I thought I'd seen the last of her, but I'd been wrong. She'd turned up at odd moments but on a regular basis, and here she was again like a bee buzzing around an opened pop can, snooping around for an opening. I lifted my head off crossed arms and glared up at her. The library was proving to not be the haven I'd hoped it would be.

"No," I said.

"Sure you do. C'mon. Her aunt Mel wants to meet you. She loves that wolf. It's hanging in the kitchen window, just like I predicted."

"Good. Great. Leave me alone."

"So she wants to thank you in person. The artist." She grinned. "And plus, she's Metis, just like you probably are, so maybe you'd feel like talking to her or something. She's really good to talk to. I've learned a ton about Metis stuff lately."

When I didn't respond, she looked at me appraisingly. "Well," she said, "actually that's pretty much a total lie. I haven't learned anything. I've been hanging with Deena is all. She's Metis like her aunt, and the weird thing is they never ever act all high and mighty or like I'm a total loser or anything. Which is very cool when you stop to think about it. You know," she prodded. "You guys have tons of history and all that stuff, and I'm just ordinary."

"Look," I tried reasoning, knowing all along it probably was not going to work, but trying all the same to keep this girl at a distance, "I am not Metis. I don't see why you keep bugging me about it. I'm not anything. Not an artist, either. I'm just a guy in high school. That's it."

"Yeah, well, she wants to meet you anyway." Ari tugged at my sleeve and I jerked my arm away. "Whatcha got to do that's so important anyway? Probably nothing, right? So, c'mon!

"Plus I want you to meet Eric. I need a male perspective." She looked me over critically. "You'll do," she said shortly.

Against my better judgment I just had to ask. "Who's Eric?"

"My boyfriend. Except he's not. Not really." Ari twisted her hands in front of her and then burst out, "OK, I wish he was my boyfriend. I think he's so cute! But he's so, I dunno, so out there and weird. Half the time, you don't know if he's listening or dreaming or living in some fantasy world. It's so frustrating!"

Ah. Perfect. More crazy people. Just what I needed. "No," I said again.

"Look." Her voice dropped to a whisper. "If you don't come see her then I don't think I can stop what's gonna happen."

In spite of myself I was intrigued. Just how far was this girl willing to go to show her interest in me? It wasn't unusual exactly, since in my experience girls are pretty easy to impress, but the person I'd thought of as shy little Ari was proving to be more aggressive than most. Making up an imaginary 'boyfriend' to get my attention. Not exactly original thinking, but at the same time it was flattering. And then to cook up a mysterious 'happening' with implied threat. For some reason I was feeling indulgent. It might be kind of cool to hear her rave over my work and to see the piece hanging in some stranger's house.

"OK, fine," I said. "I'll come see the aunt."

"Great! Cool!" She was ecstatic. "Awesome! Because if you didn't, then knowing my mother the way I do, she'd be wandering over here unasked and unwanted, and believe me you do not want that to happen."

Her mother? How did this become about anyone's mother?

"What?" I was a little bummed. "What happened to the mysterious boyfriend you wanted advice about?"

"Oh, him. Yeah, I still want a male perspective. Eric." Her eyes went all dreamy and I slammed my book shut. "Yes," she said, apparently startled, "yes, I do want your opinion. And Mel wants to thank you in person. That's actually the main thing. Eric might not even be there. He works a lot."

There was still the little remark about random mothers showing up. The last thing I needed or wanted was more mothers hanging around. My own was enough. Her behaviour, if anything, had become odder in such obscure ways I often couldn't even be sure if she was being odd or not. Maybe it was me, not her.

"What was all that stuff about your mother?" I was suspicious, and I figured my suspicion was justified.

"Nothing. Well, just that she's been reading the stories in the paper, and I told her you made the stained glass thing and she's always more than ready to nurture like a madwoman. Nurturing is her thing, so to speak, and she's got this huge conscience, she's like a rolling giant Mother Earth Woman, and she's always wanting to meet my friends, even though I told her we weren't exactly friends, at least not yet."

She paused finally to suck in some air. "So I told her you were gonna meet Mel and she thought that was cool. I put her off your trail." She grinned at me. "You can thank me later," she added grandly.

11

Walking into the little house Deena shared with her aunt Mel was like entering a place I'd been waiting to find and wanting to find, but avoiding and not even knowing I was avoiding it, all at the same time. Letting Ari talk me into meeting this woman was starting to feel like one of those dumb decisions I knew I'd regret later, and wish I'd never made in the first place, but at this point with the three of us walking down the street together it was too late to crap out on the whole idea.

What Ari didn't get was that all I really wanted was to be left alone. I wanted peace and quiet, a concept Ari herself had probably never heard of in her life. She was turning out to be one of the most aggravatingly talkative people I'd ever met. She just didn't seem to ever stop. She's a bit like a custom t-top '63 Corvette, a very cool-looking car which you think would be absolutely great to drive, but maybe the thing's been sitting in a barn somewhere for 40 years and now the brakes are faulty and the body looks good, but the under-the-hood stuff has never been maintained. That's what Ari's like. She isn't exactly a car, obviously, she's not even remotely cool and in addition to that Ari's verbal brakes don't exist, but otherwise the car analogy stands.

Deena's house was a very old one-storey structure fronted by a tiny cedar-plank porch hunkered down, as if trying to protect itself, on a ragged inner city lot. It was covered in splintery white wide-cut wooden siding faded from weather and time and desperate for a new coat of paint. The mossy shingles were starting to peel on one corner of the roof, making the roof look like it was moulting. A couple of ancient pine trees framed the yard, towering over the tiny place like a protective green smokescreen, their bulging roots making a hilly imprint on the beaten grass. The last remnants of the winter's snow still sat in dirty patches over the roots, where wisps of bright green spring grass were beginning to poke through. On the corner next to the house was an abandoned lot facing out onto a busy road and tangled with drifts of old newspaper and broken beer bottles. There was a graffitied bus stop in front of the lot, the seat busted up and Plexiglas sides dented.

Ari was still talking, extolling for my benefit the virtues of that guy she liked, when Deena cracked open a rickety back screen door and an impression of shabby comfort poured out at us. Inside, the little house seemed bigger than it actually was, and with afternoon sunlight pouring through clean windows the entry and kitchen were bright and warm. The house itself, once we finally got inside, was a cozy-feeling place with a friendly vibe to it. Cozy can sometimes slide pretty quickly into claustrophobic, but the mood the place sent out relaxed me enough to let me slightly drop my guard for a couple of minutes. It felt kind of good to drop my guard, to be honest.

For some reason it felt very easy and comfortable kicking my shoes off onto the pile by the wall before following Ari and Deena up the short set of steps to the kitchen. Although I'd never been there before, Mel and the house itself seemed familiar somehow, and a piece of me that had been searching all my life, without my even realizing it, found the space it'd been looking for.

There's also no good way of explaining how antsy and itchy the emotions sparked by the place made me feel, and how badly I wanted to get out of there. Now. It was a crazy feeling, but something I couldn't just ignore. Getting out as quick as possible was not an option; it was mandatory. No being polite. No talking. No visiting and getting to know any of them. I needed to get the hell out.

"Hey there." The voice that greeted us was quiet, but held a note of command.

I followed Ari and Deena to the top of the stairs to see a woman standing with one hip braced against the kitchen counter, her arms crossed, waiting for a kettle on the stove to heat. "I'm Mel," she continued. She was smiling at all of us, but speaking to me. "I'm Deena's aunt. You must be James."

I nodded. "I've heard about you," she said.

"Uh, yeah," I mumbled. Smooth as always. "Nice to meet you."

Deena's aunt turned out to be one of those people whose eyes seem to look straight out, unflinching, at the world, whose radar vision sees right through you. Without actually asking questions or forcing conversation, I had the impression she knew who I was, and not just my name, but who I was inside the name. She seemed ready to simply stay silent if that was what I wanted or to listen and share, depending on where I wanted this thing to go. Like a chameleon, she was reading the situation, adapting to it and ready to accept me on my own terms. To be honest, it freaked me out.

"Come in." She waved an arm, welcoming me into her kitchen, keeping her eyes on me. Dark brown eyes that didn't give anything away. As I continued to stand near the stairs, she pointed to a chair and added, "Sit down."

Which I did, and then felt so completely out of my element and so foreign and tense, I immediately stood up again. Mel watched me without comment or a change in expression.

While I stood there, unsure of what to do, I took the time to get a look at her, and size her up the way she was doing with me. She seemed a lot younger than she probably was, judging by the grey strands in her long braid of hair. She wore a red T-shirt, with the word 'Freedom' scrawled in blue across the top of a swimming tortoise, worn jeans with the cuffs turned up, and a pair of light-brown beaded moccasins.

"Tea?" she asked, watching me watch her, and when I nodded she took down another cup and placed it on the table where Ari and Deena were already sitting. They were eyeing us with interest, quiet for once. Both of them had kept up an endless stream of commentary on the way over—Ari in particular, who had rambled on and on about the guy she was hot over until I was sick of hearing about him and his friggin' heart-throbbing ways. The silence felt restful.

Mel swung her long braid back over one shoulder and looked over at me where I still stood, silent and uncomfortable. "Don't want to sit?"

"Nope."

"OK." She sat down at the table, and began filling cups from the teapot in front of her. "I like the wolf." She nodded at the kitchen window where the stained glass that formed the moon was catching the last rays of the afternoon sun and glowing in yellow swirls like a golden orb.

"Uh, yeah." I nodded. "Good," I said.

She watched me for a long minute while I tried to find any place other than her face to focus my attention. "Your tea will get cold."

I fumbled at a chair and sat down.

"Ari told me about you making it. Real nice." She took a long sip.

"Thanks." I held my mug of scalding tea and tried to drink without burning my mouth.

My only thought was to get this whole lame gratitude for the wolf procedure done and over with and get out of there. I had a frozen block of something nasty lodged deep inside me and a choice of either listening to it and behaving like a jerk to this woman, or swallowing the fear and pride and letting myself soften up. I chose to keep the blockage. At least I knew the blockage. I understood the blockage. If I let it go, I didn't know who or what I'd be anymore; it was a choice for change, and I wasn't ready to make it.

Ari was sitting on the other side of the table sipping away at her tea, nibbling on cheese and crackers and completely oblivious to how uneasy I was. She watched me distantly, like someone watching a stranger making a fool of himself. As if this wasn't all her fault in the first place. And that thought ticked me off.

"So." I stood again and put my nearly full cup back on the table. "I gotta go."

"What? Already? Why?" Ari was startled out of her silence. "What about what you promised?"

" I never made any promises," I reminded her gruffly.

"Yeah, OK, no promises," she said, "but I thought you wanted to get to know Mel. And Eric. You hardly even *said* anything."

Deena rolled her eyes and Mel cradled her cup, keeping to herself.
"Ari, listen," I began.

"No, c'mon!" she insisted. "I told you you'd like them and I know
they'll like you. They can help with all the stuff around you and how
messed-up you are. And, plus, like I told you, Mel's Metis, too. Like
you and Deena. So that should count for something! Y'know, ties
that bind and shared ancestors and history and all that stuff."

"What are you saying?" I shot back, stung by her ridiculous
assumptions. "You're talking about ancestors and history and crap
like that? Think, Ari! Who were your ancestors? They were probably German or, I dunno, Irish or something like that. So what does
that make you?"

This girl had a way of making me nuts with her crazy logic that
made sense only to her.

"Scottish, I'll have you know," she replied coldly. She raised her
pointy chin in the air and carried on. "And possibly Norse. Probably
my ancient aunts and grandmothers were pillaged by the Vikings.
It's highly likely."

The rage in me was building, and even though I realized it was
pointless to try to reason with her, I snarled back, "And so of course
you wear a crazy horned hat, and a kilt and play bagpipes and hang
around with other people who have Scottish grandparents! Don't
be such an idiot, Ari! You are what you are and I am what I am, and
all those ancient ancestors have absolutely nothing to do with life
today. Nothing."

She was silent for a second, which is probably a record in her
case, and then veered off without warning, like she always does,
into a completely different subject.

"And Eric's not here yet, either," she said. "You have to hang
around 'til he gets here at least. You said you'd check him out for
me. Kinda like a brother or something. You promised!"

She glared over at me, every hair on her head seeming to bristle
upright and vibrate with the potency of her indignation. And then
suddenly she deflated and sagged back against her chair before her
attention turned yet again to an entirely different and totally unwel-
come direction.

Her voice slowed and sank lower. "They won't be around you forever, y'know." She sounded calmer, more rational, with every word she spoke. She was gazing steadily at something behind my right shoulder. "Not unless you want them to," she said.

"Ari, knock it off!" She was annoying the hell out of me. But I was a long ways past being only annoyed; I was royally pissed. And more than a little creeped out. I had no firm idea of who 'they' were, but a part of me already knew and didn't want that knowledge.

She ignored me, of course. As usual. And continued, which was no surprise either. "There are smoky barriers, like very thin curtains, and we can move through them, but it's not easy. It takes a kind of energy and will; it takes concentration and intention. You have to want it."

I glanced around, wondering if these women were always this weird, but Deena was calmly drinking her tea and Mel's eyes were gazing at the tree branches behind the window.

"There are some people you just don't say goodbye to," Ari said in that same monotonous voice that was seriously getting on my nerves. "Maybe it's because wherever you are there's a piece of them there, too. They haunt your dreams; they walk beside you during the day."

"Shut up." My voice was hoarse in the quiet kitchen. "Just shut up."

If there's one thing that really upsets me it's standing out in any kind of crowd, and these three women made up one creepy, unmanageable crowd in my mind. Not only that, but it was weird and a little sinister how Ari's voice changed like that, since she's normally one of those goofy talkative chicks who goes on and on about any dumb thing that catches her attention and who you just wish would shut up once in a while. Deena and Mel were not helping any either; both were sitting there silently sipping tea as if this kind of thing was a normal occurrence, which maybe it was in their world, but it definitely was not in mine.

I was standing there like some kind of idiot, next to my chair, uncertain what to do next, feeling like such a dope, and then I couldn't seem to stop myself.

"What are you talking about?" I asked, already aware that I shouldn't ask anything, but should just get up and walk out.

"You can choose whether you want this in your life or whether you want to shut it down." Ari spoke slowly, deliberately, still in that slightly eerie voice that made me grit my teeth with exasperation. "But you should *choose*, not just let it happen to you. Decide. And you can un-decide later if you want, but it'll be tougher to find them again once you toss it all away."

For a second I could almost feel steam coming out of the top of my head because I was so outraged by her seeming to assume she knew what was good for me. Nobody ever gave this girl the right to think she knew anything about me. And there was absolutely no reason for her to think I needed help from anyone. Who and what the hell was she talking about anyway? Who asked her? Before all this happened, all she'd been was another girl in the school halls; she'd meant nothing to me or I to her and *now*, well now she had become a major pain in the butt. And I had never asked for that.

"I don't want any help from you or anyone else." I pushed the chair I'd used back under the table and took a step backward. This had to end here. "And being Metis or not being Metis has nothing to do with anything. And there's nobody, not one single person, behind me or around me. You don't know me!" And for a moment I just stood there, helpless, my arms at my sides.

"Leave me alone," I said into the silence. The words probably came out a lot louder than I intended them to. "All of you can just friggin' leave me the hell alone! I'm not interested in being a born-again Metis, no offence Mel. And quit thinking that being Metis is all I am, Ari!" I was shooting out at random, but I was hitting my marks. "And I'm not looking for anyone's help, no matter who they are. I don't need you people in my life, pushing your attitudes and ideas onto me!"

Ari's meddling had finally been the spark that sent me into orbit. My defences were worn down after everyone's interference in my life, and even though I hate getting angry at anyone, and even though I'd usually rather die than have everybody's eyes on me, at this point I couldn't seem to help myself. It doesn't happen often, but when I get mad I tend to blow like popped cork, which is one reason I like keeping a really low profile and holding my feelings inside where nobody else has access and I don't have any awkward explaining to do.

But this was just too much. I already had a mother whose invasive behaviour had become so hit-and-miss and unpredictable, it sometimes took all the patience I could drag out of myself just to deal with her without losing my temper. And even though it was just her and me and nobody else, no aunts or grandparents or anything, I also knew I didn't want or need anyone else. I certainly didn't need or want any adopted 'Aunts' like Mel. Or anyone else's mother for that matter. No matter how messed-up Mom was, she was mine and we stuck together. No matter what happened, or how bad things got, it was her and me, and we were in it for the long haul.

And this life I was living was *my* dream or *my* nightmare and nobody else's. I was determined not to be defined by my skin colour or by my parents and their backgrounds and their racial characteristics and their demons. Determined to be defined by me and only me. Rooster. James. Whatever I am called. But at all costs to not think of myself as first and foremost a man of any race other than the human race. And I won't be lonely. And I will never give up.

Leaving the house that day, I almost ran down the block. I flew out of there like a sparrow out of a tree full of hungry cats.

12

And that's when my long phase of avoidance began. Avoiding Ari at school, turning my back whenever Deena happened to wander by, making sure not to catch anyone else's eyes, and keeping myself to my own self no matter what. I steered clear of any mention, any reminder, any hint of the previous existence of Jen and Frank.

The only thing I couldn't seem to prevent coming into my head was the memory of that kitchen with Mel in it so quiet and watchful, and the warmth of the place, but that memory was easy to turn off once it showed up. Mel's world was not mine, and I knew I could never be a part of it. Didn't even want to be a part of it. My world consisted of school, Mom, my own demons and nobody else. I was on a solo journey. Life was pretty empty, and as far as dealing with Mom was concerned, I learned to simply turn and walk away from her when she started drinking and crying after dinner. I closed my door, dropped to the floor, leaned back against my bed, and inserted earphones.

Looking back, it was a dark time. It seems when I think about it, that the sun never shone, the days never brightened. It was always night—a night without stars or moon.

That wasn't the actual case of course, because spring had arrived, the sun was warm and the days were longer, the snow melted and people began coming out of their cocoons. The grass, flowers and birds all got busy doing what they do best. But for me, the entire world was overshadowed by darkness and clouds, a threatening nothingness.

And even though it sounds selfish and stupid, I kept thinking all that 'why me?' crap, as in 'why was it me left behind?' and 'how come it's me who has to suffer all this pain and always be alone?' and sometimes just, 'why?'. In some ways, because I was so lost and alone, it was as if it was I who was dead and not only Jen and Frank. It was a hole I couldn't seem to dig myself out of.

Thinking those thoughts, even though they came at me unawares and I didn't think them on purpose, just knowing I had thoughts like that made me feel not only bitter, but also as if I hated myself as much as I hated what happened to them. All I could do was pull into myself, like some crazy guy hiding in a cave, and keep the rest of the world out there in its careless golden sunshine, away from me. Away from all the hurt inside.

And it worked. For a while.

That strategy of avoidance began falling apart when Mom informed me one evening she'd be driving me to school every morning starting the next day. She wasn't planning to listen to any reasoning I came up with, and the subject, according to her, was closed. It was a done deal.

"James, I know you've been missing school," she said after dinner, "and that's not a good thing. It's got to stop."

"Yeah." I was slouched on the sofa, flipping elastic bands across the living room, not really listening, but ready to agree with whatever she had to say in order to avoid arguing with her.

"I'm serious, James," she insisted. Her back was to me and she bent down to touch the leaves of one of her houseplants. "Dry," she mumbled to herself. "Really dry. How do these plants get so dry so quick? I'm sure I watered them yesterday!"

When I didn't respond, she stood and stared back over her shoulder at me. Her eyes were dark and unreadable in the early-evening shadows of the living room. "We leave at 7:30 sharp. Be ready."

"I'll take the bus."

"No. Oh, no. You've been taking the bus these past months, and evidently that's all you've been doing."

She bent again to test the soil of her houseplant. She picked a couple of dried leaves off and crumbled them in her hand, letting the remains fall onto the coffee table. "Huh," she said. "So dry. I just don't understand how it gets so dry."

"Mom," I began, "I'll go to school. Honest."

"Honest-shmonest. Your principal called me today. Do you have any idea how embarrassing it was to be asked where you've been for the last two weeks? I had no idea. I thought they knew where you were." She shook a long finger at me. "It's going to stop. Right here. Right now."

"Fine." I stood and left the room, heading for my bed and some music. "Drive me if you want. Go ahead." I knew I sounded like a little teenage chump, but at that point I didn't care. I was pissed. Being driven to school like a six year old. Ridiculous.

It had become apparent to me that I wasn't learning anything at school anymore, and therefore I didn't see much point in sticking around and pretending to learn all the junk they said we needed to learn. At the same time it had evidently became apparent to her, thanks no doubt to some teacher interference, that I was not attending any of my classes.

But what nobody seemed to get was how I knew it was a waste of my time to sit there in school while people talked and tried to get me to become involved in life again, and even more than just a waste of my time, it was also a waste of their time. They must all have had more important stuff to do with their days than sit and talk at a guy when he's not even remotely listening. And I wasn't listening, because it had become crystal clear to me that none of it, absolutely nothing they said, mattered. A concept that nobody else seemed to understand. How, when peoples' lives can end so suddenly and so unfairly, when they can simply disappear off the face of the earth without any warning or any goodbyes, how could anyone possibly still insist that math concepts or science labs matter in the least?

The habit of skipping had started with me heading off to school one morning, just like normal, and then, without even consciously deciding not to go in that day, making a hard right turn at the entrance and walking instead six blocks to the downtown mall. Wandering around stores that were selling things I didn't want, looking at the blank, barren faces around me of people shopping for stuff they didn't need, I watched the office workers come crawling out of their towers like so many ants at coffee break and lunchtime, and all of it only served to emphasize how pointless life really was.

All the striving, the hustling for good grades so I could get into some kind of post-secondary school and all the working summers to save up for a potential reward somewhere far down the line of my pathetic life. It was all a total waste. There was nobody to travel with anymore. Nobody to trade jokes and talk about what we wanted to do with our lives and how we'd always be friends and live in the same neighbourhood as each other. Frank and I had even decided our future wives would be friends. We'd make sure our kids all played on the same teams. Maybe we'd coach our kids together. Both of us could see it all so clear. All those dreams and plans had died with the avalanche that smothered Frank. There was nothing left.

Even Mom, the person closest to me now, didn't get it. She figured she'd simply lay down the law and I'd obey without question. Where she gets her ideas from I'll never know. In her head, it was obvious if she drove me to school, dropped me at the front entrance, and watched me walk up the steps and through the front doors, her job was done. I was where I was supposed to be, and I'd stay there all day and then meet her at home again at night. Business as usual. She didn't see any other options.

What never seemed to enter her mind was that I could escape the place any time I felt like it. Sometimes I'd wave at her when she drove off, then I'd hit my first class and take off again after the second-class bell. Sometimes I'd stick around for my crafts class, fiddle with the glass and do some soldering, then take off for the rest of the after-noon. It was pretty haphazard—whatever I figured I needed to do. And the teachers and staff somehow let it happen, probably thinking I'd had enough to deal with this year. But the last thing I wanted was for anyone to treat me like a special case; I'd have respected them more if they'd come down on me like they normally would have. I could've used a good bawling out in front of the entire class.

Thing is, the ability to escape class and wander the city really wasn't what I wanted anyway, even though with spring now in full force, it was nice to be outside and making my way through the city streets. What I really needed was a place to belong—an anchor, something to hang onto and something to rage away at. I needed something to hit.

13

That freedom from a normal schedule, even though it was a stolen kind of freedom, is how I eventually found myself hanging out in Blues Inverted. A bar known throughout the city for bringing in various blues bands from around the country and for the eclectic clientele it attracts, it operates out of a crappy little ancient hotel called the Royal, down on Crimson Street.

Since I wasn't sleeping much and food didn't appeal in any way, I was skinnier than ever, but I also had tons of energy. A lot more than normal. Go figure. It made no sense, but I could walk for miles and most days I did, from school in the north of downtown, past the office towers and south through the river valley to the University area and Crimson Street.

Crimson's a shopping area dominated by music shops, little boutiques and other stores that are seemingly designed specifically to encourage women to spend money. Jen had loved the area. There's an antique movie theatre and a bunch of bars and restaurants. It's good people-watching all year round, and in the summer there are a whole whack of festivals and street performers. They close the street down and hold outdoor markets with crafts and foods. Frank and I used to go hang there for the entertainment value of just looking at the girls walk by.

On the day I ended up at the bar, I'd left school in mid-morning and walked the five miles down to Crimson, just to wander and watch. I hadn't counted on running into anyone I knew there, and when I recognized Mel window-shopping her way down the sidewalk, I ducked into a music store and made my way through the stacks to the back of the place, hoping she'd pass by and I'd go unnoticed.

Of course that didn't happen. Naturally. It figured that Mel would be out shopping for CDs, not clothing, and when she entered the front door, and turned to her right, heading down the roots music aisle, I scootched down a little behind the jazz section, and began duck-walking my way to the front of the store. She browsed her way past roots, picking up a CD now and then and putting it back, moving into the R&B section, her head down, scanning titles.

A grizzled old clerk at the front of the store, a guy who looked like he'd seen more than his share of shoplifters, frowned as he watched me waddle past jazz and slip into the aisle between country and hip hop. When he started out from behind the desk and it looked like he was going to blow my cover, I gestured wildly over at Mel and made a throat-slashing move at him. He stopped short, and shook his head at me before grinning a gap-toothed smile, probably reliving his own school-skipping activities back in the day.

Taking a turn past rockabilly, he walked over to stand beside Mel, and then started up a conversation with her about the CD she was holding. That move gave me the chance I needed to sneak my way past the rows of CDs and out the front door again. The old guy was pretty cool about it all. Probably figured she was my mother and I was AWOL from school, which was half true anyway. Terrified she'd come out of the store, spot me and insist on actually carrying on a conversation, I trotted down the sidewalk to the nearest open door and slid my way in.

That open door led into Blues Inverted, where a jam session was beginning to set up on the little stage. After dark there's always someone at the door, as I know now, checking ID and making sure nobody enters the place who's drunk, dangerous or underage, but on a bright spring afternoon like that one the door was open, the ticket booth empty and I walked from the sunny street into a shadowed interior, hardly able to see my hand in front of my eyes.

The rank smell of ancient cigarette smoke hit me first, embedded as it was in the walls and beer-stained carpet, and I coughed while still trying to keep what I hoped would be an extremely low profile.

The walls were a yellowy white colour, with old televisions broadcasting silent sports events, hanging haphazardly at intervals. An odd scent of old cat-piss permeated the air. At least I was assuming that was what stale cat-piss might smell like, since it stunk like nothing else I'd ever smelled before, although how old cats with bladder issues ever got in the place was anybody's guess.

Blues Inverted is the type of place they write sad, down-on-your-luck songs about. It draws the kind of clientele most people look at as some kind of freak show. Old bikers with old biker chicks, young bikers accompanied by even younger biker chicks, and artists, musicians and people who generally don't give a rat's ass about what others might think, make up the majority of the regulars there. It's a place whose mandate is to play blues music and only the blues, with an emphasis on all that 'my baby left me for my best friend on his motorcycle and now she's sorry and wants to come back but my broken heart can't be mended that easy' kind of riff going for it.

That was my first afternoon in the place, but in the future I'd find out you could be down and depressed about just about anything and still write a song about it. Most of the time the lyrics involved women, of course. Women, old trucks, motorcycles and sometimes a dog. Hound dogs more often than, say, labs or bulldogs, and always old dogs. Never did hear a song involving a poodle, but I guess it could happen because song lyrics could get pretty personal. One afternoon a guy from Winnipeg worked his way through an entire three-verse tune about the emotional impact of seeing his ex-girlfriend's reflection in the hubcap of his '67 Cadillac when she strolled past with her new boyfriend.

There are endless variations of broken-hearted refrains, as I eventually learned. Ones that involve the true love a guy can feel for his truck, others that hold fast to the concept of mossy trees drooping over slow-moving rivers with alluring but emotionally volatile ladies along the riverbanks, and still others that describe gritty streets and tough but vulnerable women with warm and hardened hearts that are worth the agony it takes to capture them.

The old, rundown hotel that houses Blues Inverted is the sort of place that's continually posting handwritten ads up on their walls, looking for cleaners and chambermaids, since anyone with any kind of other options ditches the place as soon as possible, moving on to cleaning up more mainstream hotels. The kind of hotels that don't attract the sort of never-ending grey grime that covers the walls, ceilings, floor and every square inch of the Royal Hotel. The type of guck the staff there would be asked to clean up didn't even bear thinking about, and I'm a pretty strong-stomached guy.

It's the sort of place where rooms rent by the hour or the night for a real low rate, sometimes just whatever the renter can cough up at the time. It's pretty slummy and grimy even in the lobby, and imagining what the rooms must be like is not a pleasant experience. Admittedly, I'm a little anal about clean sheets, my own towel, and stuff like that, and thinking about the rooms, and what goes on in them, made the place more than a little disgusting, but at the same time the music was good on the day I ended up there and the grunginess of the place didn't affect me much.

I tried to look like I belonged and made my way past the pool tables and bar to the even darker, windowless side of the room, where people who looked like they'd been born in the place were pulling chairs to the little scarred wooden tables, in order to sit with friends.

The only empty table was near the washrooms, giving me a great view of everyone, since the washrooms seemed to be the most popular part of the place. People sped in there in obvious need, only to wander out a few minutes later, looking relieved and ready for more beer. They stood in little groups, greeting old friends, passing around hugs and slaps on the back like they'd found long-lost buddies from years past.

"What'll you have?" A tall, skinny girl was standing in front of my table, holding a tray full of empties, and looking down at me. Taken by surprise, I sat a little straighter and tried to make it appear as if I was of legal age and hung out in bars all the time. Thing is, the legal age was still a year or so away for me, and she could probably tell.

"Hey, kid," she said, "its time to get going. C'mon, out you go."

"Listen." I was desperate to not get thrown out. Not by a girl, at least. "Listen, I'm just here . . ."

"Just here for what?" She snapped her gum and put the tray on my table as if carrying it around had just got to be too much for her. She put her hands on her hips. "What're you here for?"

Having random girls call me on stuff isn't something I necessarily look forward to, but right then it seemed like her possibly making fun of me was better than her getting mad. She wore a very short black skirt, a tiny black T-shirt a couple of sizes too small and high black boots made out of some cheap, shiny synthetic material. Around one bicep she had a tattoo of a couple of snakes twined together. Bar keys and an ID card were on a chain around her neck. Her long blonde hair was tied back in a ponytail, and she pushed at her bangs and rubbed one eye while she waited for me to speak. She looked like she didn't put up with much crap.

"I'm trying to avoid someone. Out there." I motioned toward the front of the place. "I just wanna stay for a few minutes. Please," I added as an afterthought.

"Old girlfriend?" She grinned down at me and I realized she was probably a lot older than I'd thought. She was no girl anymore. The laugh lines were a giveaway.

"No. A friend's aunt." It came out in a rush, and if you asked me now why I was so honest then, I'd have to say I have no friggin' idea. I was honest with her because I couldn't think of anything else to say or do. I was brain-dead, basically. Telling the truth was my only option. "She's gonna want to talk to me and make everything all better for me, and I can't face her or those other crazy girls who hang at her place."

She laughed aloud and shook her head at me. "No shit," she said. "I figured there'd be women involved in your problem. You're kinda cute."

There was a pause while she snapped her gum and stretched her back out. Then she obviously reached a conclusion of some kind, and said, "Listen, if anyone asks, just say you're with the band. Nobody'll know. No ordering booze, though, got it?"

"Yeah. Yeah, for sure, I've got it."

She picked up her tray again with a sigh at its weight. "I'll bring you a Coke," she said, heading to the guys at the table behind me.

Which is when things suddenly took a nosedive into worse than I'd thought they could get, because Mel strolled into the front of the room, waved at the bartenders, hugged a couple of the waitresses and stepped up onto the stage, all before I could even think about making a break for it.

"Hey, everybody!" The mic squealed and she waved at the guy on the soundboard. "Hey, everyone!" she tried again.

"Welcome to the open mic at Blues Inverted!" She threw her arms up and waved into the crowd. The emcee, naturally. Some days there's just no luck but bad luck.

A wall of sound opened up as the assorted audience members stood and whooped and clapped. Seemed this was a popular place to be. I stayed in my seat, my main goal being to escape any sort of notice, not just from Mel but also from anyone else, particularly the bartenders, who looked like they'd worked their way through more than one bar fight, and from the bouncers, who looked even tougher. One of them stood near the ladies' washroom, his back to the door, narrowed eyes continuously scanning the place. He wore a knit hat over a shaved head, a black T-shirt with the bar's logo on it, black jeans, biker boots and an expression of withering disgust. The way his arms bulged out of the sleeves of his shirt made me acutely aware of the importance of a low profile.

"I don't know why this corner of the place is so crowded." The waitress was back and she was crabby, yelling at me over the racket. "It just feels so tight in here. There's hardly room to move."

Tight? I glanced around. Unless she was talking about the ghostly companions Ari saw around me—and I grinned silently to myself, knowing how ridiculous the notion was—then I had no idea what she was referring to.

Two grizzled old guys sat at the table on my right. They were screaming at each other over the music, but since, in addition to the noise from the band and the other patrons, they were probably both stone deaf, their conversation wasn't going far. Each of them was poking a bony forefinger at the other, making a point about something important, and the veins in their necks stuck out as they hollered away about the sleazy habits of the ex-wife of one of them.

There was nobody behind or to the other side of me. Hard to see why she was complaining about the crowds.

"So stuffy and thick," she said, plonking a glass on my table. While I fished in my jeans for coins, she continued, "Listen, if you want to blend in, if you want the manager to think you're just another roadie, you better learn to drink that crap we call coffee. It's free for the talent, and they drink it by the gallon. Probably one reason a lot of 'em die young." She laughed at her own joke, exposing dimples and a missing tooth on the right side of her mouth.

Suddenly uneasy at her attention, and hoping nobody else noticed her standing there talking to me, I passed her some coins, enough for a small tip, in the hope she'd leave. She looked down at me with a thoughtful expression and then sighed.

"I talked to the manager about you," she said, and I must have looked a little jumpy at the news, because she added quickly, "Gotta cover my own rear, y'know. Anyway, he said as long as you stay quiet, listen to the music, don't get in trouble and do *not*," she said emphatically, "do not attempt to order booze, you're OK."

"OK. Yup. Got it." I was pretty relieved to know the big bouncer at the ladies' washroom was staying put. There wasn't any immediate danger of him strolling over and hurling me headfirst out on the sidewalk. A huge sense of gratitude washed over me and I grinned up at the girl before she left.

"Cheers," I said, raising my glass, suddenly feeling more upbeat than I had in weeks. "Wanna have a drink with me when you get off your shift later? Maybe a beer or something? Not for me, of course, but for you," I added when she frowned. "Y'know, just sit and talk or something?"

"You're cute," she said, "but a little on the young side." One corner of her mouth curled up and she added, "I'll come and have a coffee later on if you're still here, OK?"

"Yeah, sure!" And I practically fell all over myself showing how glad I was she'd smoothed things out for me. "That'd be great!"

Against all odds, the place was starting to grow on me even in that short period of time. It was dark, and insanely grubby, and by the way my glass stuck to the table, I figured it was safe to assume there was a lot of nasty stuff on the table and floor, which was probably better I not know about. And the room was filled with some pretty sketchy kinds of people. All the same, I found myself beginning to already like a bunch of the people. The old geezers next to me, for example. They looked like they could be pretty entertaining if somebody sat down with them and helped them hear what each other was saying.

Also, the guy who'd taken to the stage was starting to sound kind of good and I wanted to stay and listen longer. He was pretty old himself, with long grey hair hanging limply over his shoulders, and the tightest blue jeans on a pair of the skinniest legs I ever saw on anyone in my life. His worn-out cowboy boots looked like they'd done some shit-kicking in their day and he wore them with his jeans tucked in so the boots with scrolled stitching up the outsides kind of grabbed your eye. He wore a baseball cap and an old flannel shirt.

He looked more like a down-and-out country singer or an old wino, but he sang blues. Nothing but blues. And he sang from the heart of some rich dregs of sorrow. If you listened to him with your eyes closed, you'd swear you were listening to some old guy in Mississippi or New Orleans the way he sang about dark smoky swamps and beautiful ladies who let their men down in a heartless way. It wasn't really my kind of music, but it was good all the same, and I sat back in my chair, kept myself quiet and spent the rest of the afternoon into the early evening watching the various customers around me and making sure Mel stayed over there on the stage, away from my side of the place and unaware of my presence.

14

Mom yanked at the wheel, swerved sharply and launched the car into the school parking lot, cutting off a city transit bus as she did so, bumping up over the curb and into the entry lane, narrowly missing another vehicle before she slid into a space and turned and glared over at me. A couple of empty coffee go-cups bounced up onto the seat and I knocked them back down to the floor to mix with the scraps of paper and trash on the floor mats.

It was a couple of days after my discovery of Blues Inverted, and because I'd been a little late coming home that day, she was still riled up and dangerously emotional. Somehow she'd got the idea in her head that night while she waited supper for me that I'd run away from home or something, and when I showed up later, the fireworks began. They involved tears, hysterics, raised voices and manic hugs full of apologies. It was wild. But not as wild as the ride to school this morning.

My face must have registered my terror and my hands were still clenched on the armrest at my seat. "Holy crap!" I shouted.

"What?" Her voice was flat, emotionless.

I was silent for a second, not only disturbed by what she'd just done, but also still a little scared for my life. My pathetic life, which sometimes I wished would just end, but mostly still valued.

"What the hell was that?" I found my voice and it filled the car. Her driving was ridiculously dangerous and it filled me with fury. Maybe she didn't care about her own life, but she ought to care about mine and any strangers who happened to be on local sidewalks. She'd been growing more careless as the days went on, but I'd put it down to her anger at having to leave the house earlier in order to drive me to school every morning before heading off to work. I never thought she'd try to kill us. It was absolutely friggin' crazy.

"Mom, I thought that bus was gonna T-bone us for sure! What is the matter with you? Slow down! This is insane!"

"What? Why?" And now she seemed genuinely confused at my reaction. "There's absolutely nothing wrong with my driving!" she continued in a huffy tone. "I have been driving since long before you were even born. They taught us defensive driving in those days, which is something you young people have no idea about. I'm an excellent driver. My marks were highest in my class!"

And now in addition to being baffled by my obvious fear she was also rapidly becoming infuriated by it. Just what I needed: more mom-style dramatics, and at school no less. Her hands were still on the steering wheel. Positioned at 10 and 2, just like in the manual, but the knuckles were growing white with tension and her voice was beginning to get that warning waver in it.

"What gives you the right," she began, staring straight ahead over the steering wheel, "to talk to me like that?"

Figuring I had one slim chance to get out of there quick, I opened the passenger door, shoved one foot out and then slumped back against the seat as she continued, her voice gathering speed and momentum. "You can just stop hounding me about every little thing, James! You go in there." She pointed at the school. "Go in that building right there. That place where you go, and you get to work! You make sure you work all day and you bring your money home again tonight. I'm sick of doing all the work and you just up and spend all the money! So get in there and when you come home you give me the cheque." She was waving a finger in my face now. "The bank manager and I have a plan. Do you understand?"

I understood all right; I understood she was crazy. I sat there with my mouth open listening to her garbled talk, and for the first time in dealing with her I felt real fear. All this time, while she talked to her plants and either forgot to water them altogether or watered them until they drowned, while she ordered four identical extra-large pizzas when one was more than enough, while she brought home hugely expensive shoes and then wore them in the snow and ruined them, all this time I'd just thought it was only Mom being weird.

Now that her bizarre actions were showing signs of being potentially hazardous I actually began to be afraid for both her and me.

Which is why that night, after she settled into the living room with a beer and the remote, I hid her car key, shoving it deep in the pocket of my jeans where she had to go through me to get at it. It was the only thing I could think of to prevent her using her car to kill herself, me, or someone else. In her hands that vehicle had become a weapon of sorts—something that might maim if we were lucky and it didn't actually take a life, but something she seemingly had no control over anymore.

The fact she seemed to be losing her memory helped with the whole crazy plan. Normally, her key ring is there in plain sight on the hook by the back door where she always leaves it, but that morning, before her terrifying drive to school, she had searched all through the house for the ring and not even seen it hanging there. Trusting that she'd be just as confused the next morning, due no doubt to her massive over-drinking at night, I figured it was safe to simply remove the ignition key from the ring and leave the house keys where they were. That way I could make sure she wasn't going to drive anywhere anytime soon, without actually having to tell her she was off the road. Hopefully this sort of subterfuge would help avoid the kind of hysterical showdown that was becoming common at our house. At least until I got things figured out.

15

"There is nothing wrong with me! Nothing!"

Mom was panting with emotion when she turned back to face me. She waved a finger in my direction before stomping past me in a sort of flat-footed dance, her feet pounding the floor. She flung open a cupboard door dramatically, and then slowly, inch by inch, and with a great show of reluctance, peered past the open door as if expecting a pair of eyes to be peering back at her.

"Nothing!" she cried again. The word was a long-drawn, almost absent howl as she stuck one hand inside the cupboard and flapped it around in a random search.

When I stayed silent she stopped for a second, out of breath from her own dramatics, and then pulled in another gasping lungful of air. We were in the kitchen the morning after I'd swiped her car key. It was early, and she'd been ransacking the house for at least 20 minutes, searching for that ignition key. Lost in a maze of fear and fury and screaming at full throttle, she was venting all her pent-up anger at me, like a little kid on the playground, striking out in random defensiveness.

"Maybe there's something wrong with you! Did you ever stop to think of that? Did you? That maybe it's you who's screwed up? Huh?"

Mom's brows were pulled together, the lines drawn deep between her glaring eyes, and for a couple of seconds, while she stood and gasped for air, I thought maybe, just maybe, she'd quiet down long enough for me to reason with her. I was wrong.

"How can you do this to me? How can you be so ungrateful? You are an ungrateful, ungrateful boy." Her mouth sagged open, drooping to one side, and she knuckled her eyes hard. "I gave you everything! I gave up everything for you!"

And then, in an instant, she was sobbing, out of control and raging in her anger and her grief. And more than that, she was afraid. Her fear was so potent it was almost like another person sharing the house with us. And I felt for her, I really did, but at the same time yesterday's terrifying drive to school was still fresh in my memory and I didn't want her killing herself or someone else with her car. There would be no way I could live with that kind of guilt if there was any way I could prevent a potential tragedy. She's my mom and I love her, no matter how crazy she gets.

"Mom, listen." I was speaking quietly like you would to a scared little animal, hoping if I kept my voice down, she'd quiet down, too. "Come on and sit down. Just relax for a minute."

I put my arm around her shoulders and began to gently steer her away from where she'd planted herself at the kitchen cupboards. She was leaning on the countertop, flipping through the remaining keys on the ring, searching desperately for that hidden car key as if she knew it had to be there on the fob where she'd left it and that somehow her eyes were just not seeing it. Forcing her across the kitchen, I pulled out a chair and sat her down at the table. Her jacket was half-off, hanging from one shoulder, and mascara was beginning to trickle in little black streams down her cheeks.

"Where is it, James? Where is my car key?" She slammed her clenched fists on the table, the remainder of the keys on the ring jangling like crazy. "Why are you *do*ing this to me?"

"Listen, Mom, maybe it's time for you to take things a little easier around here. You know, maybe slow down a little."

She glared up at me blankly, her eyes red and wet and her makeup smeared, but silent for a moment. Listening.

For some reason, I took her speechlessness as encouragement. "Driving's really stressful," I said, "so maybe just for a little while, you could take the bus to work and not drive. Or maybe take some time off work and stay home and just rest. Sleep in for a change. Do some exercising or something. Get some fresh air."

I had no concrete idea of what was happening to her, because all my life she'd been the kind of person who cried easily, whose emotions were out there raw in the breeze for everyone to see, but her recent behaviour was becoming more erratic by the day, and even a little scary, and I was basically grabbing any ideas that came into my head. She rubbed her nose hard with one fist, sniffled back tears and pushed the damp hair away from her eyes.

"James," she said. "Please. Please give me my key. Please?"

"Mom, no." There was absolutely no backing down.

She began crying again, with great wet sobs that threatened to choke her. Gasping and swallowing at her tears, she hiccuped and struggled to catch her breath. Huge salt drops brimmed up and spilled down her cheeks in what seemed like an endless stream of misery. Shoulders hunched forward, her arms curved protectively across her stomach, she gave herself totally to her outraged grief.

"Please?" Her voice broke into a whimper. "Please, honey?"

"Mom, do you remember what happened yesterday?" Sitting next to her, I was speaking as quietly and as gently as I could. I had no idea what she'd been like after dropping me off at school, and although I figured there'd probably been other close calls, I wanted to be really specific and just talk about what I knew. What she couldn't debate. "Do you remember the bus that almost hit us and how you drove up and over the curb? You scraped the bottom of the car."

She shook her head mutely. "No," she said softly.

"That bus could have killed us both. He had to slam on his brakes. Those things are big and they don't stop that easily. And that wasn't the only time, Mom. You're driving way faster than the speed limit these days, and sometimes it's like you don't see other people on the street. Or other cars either. Sometimes you're in the wrong lane."

"James, I know you took my key! I need it back. I need to go to work."

"Mom, just listen for a sec. Maybe you should stop drinking." And at the look on her face I added quickly, "Or just drink less at night. Have just one drink and stop. Maybe that'd help."

"Help how?" And again she rapidly became furious, her voice rising from relative softness into a scream. "How is that supposed to help me? I don't drink too much! I don't! And I *deserve* a drink after working all day! I work really, really hard!"

"OK," I soothed. Anything to calm her down again. "OK. You're right. You deserve a drink, but just one drink, OK? Just one? Because maybe it's the booze that's making you act this way. Just sip it slower and make it last longer."

"You are not the boss of me, James!" She sat straighter and wiped at her cheeks, rubbing the black liquid mascara further into her skin, her voice sinking once again back down to a reasonable conversational tone. "You cannot tell me what to do. I will quit when I am good and ready to quit and not one second sooner. I know what's best for me, not you. You don't know anything. You are the kid and I am the mother.

"Now," and she cleared her throat, tossed her hair back from her face, and spoke patiently, evidently finished with the conversation, "please give me my key."

Her extreme shifts in behaviour were one of the toughest things for me to understand. She could change direction so fast, going from shrill and accusatory to quiet and defensive in a heartbeat and leaving me completely unbalanced and unsure as she did so. It was like walking a tightrope over a gaping chasm while someone stood at the other end haphazardly shaking the thing.

I shook my head. "No, Mom. We can't take that chance. Someone might get hurt. *You* might get hurt."

"James!" And it began again—the shrieking voice, the tears, the dripping nose and soggy makeup, her hands raised in fists as if to beat me. "Give me my key! I'm going to be late for work! I have to get to work!"

And she hammered the table repeatedly with both fists, then raised one palm and flat-handed me across the face. Hard. Her keys were still clasped in her other hand so tightly I could see where the key teeth were cutting into her skin. My eyes had inadvertently teared up with the force of her slap, and I put my own hand on my stinging cheek.

"Fine!" I hollered back at her, my interest in dealing with her in any kind of compassionate way now completely gone. It was hopeless. "Fine! I'll get you your key and you can go out there and drive like a madwoman, take your chances, and get yourself killed some day! Is that what you want?"

I was standing then, digging into my pocket for the key, furious with the whole situation, overwhelmed by the responsibility of look-ing after her, and not only angry with her but also with myself

"Yes, James, that's what I want. I want to go to work." She dried her cheeks with the back of one hand and held the other out for her key.

"And now," she said quietly, "I am leaving. I will see you tonight."

And she left the house then with her jacket still half off, hanging from one shoulder, her cheeks darkened from the smeared rivers of mascara and her nose dripping. And to my everlasting shame, I let her go.

16

That day I actually attended school for the entire day. Took the bus, my ears still ringing from the battle with Mom, walked up the front steps and through the doors and headed to class. For the first time in weeks I went to every single class on my schedule and even took notes. Didn't participate in discussions or anything; I wasn't ready to go that far, but physically I was there, at least. One of us, I'd decided while Mom roared out of the garage and headed down the street, was going to behave like a civilized human being and it looked like that one was gonna have to be me. Mom was somewhere on another planet as far as I could tell, and expecting any kind of sense or help out of her was impossible.

That thought made me feel even lonelier than usual, lonely enough to swallow some pride, lonely enough to give things a second shot and maybe seek a little friendly support somewhere else.

"Uh." I cleared my throat and hesitated, standing like an idiot there in the hall by her locker while the rest of the school hustled around and behind me, rivers of people in waves heading out and doing their thing. "So."

Profound, I know, but it was hard knowing how to start a conversation after avoiding her for almost three weeks. Even after swearing to myself I'd never go near either her or Deena again, I found myself standing next to Ari's locker trying to act like everything was cool.

"So," she echoed. She drew herself out from rummaging around in her locker and looked up, grinning at me, her head waving around on that long neck like a flower reaching for the sun. "Hi," she said happily, as if greeting a long-lost friend.

"Hi." I was less effusive, more unsure.

"C'mon," she said, "let's go outside, it's gorgeous out there."

And she acted as if nothing had ever happened, as if nothing had come between us. It gave a huge sense of relief to the day after the incredible dramatics earlier, to have someone simply say hi and invite me along.

"Deena's waiting on the quad," Ari said. "She wanted to snag a spot before all the grassy parts are taken. I'm starved! Come sit with us and have lunch."

"Sure," I said. Out of habit, I pulled my cell out of my pocket and took it off silent mode. The menu flashed and beeped at me. "But it looks like I missed a call. A couple of calls."

"Reception is horrible in here." Ari was walking ahead of me, weaving her way through the jammed hallway, talking over her shoulder as I punched keys in my phone trying to find the missed call number. A sinking feeling was already telling me it wasn't going to be good news.

"Come outside," she added. "I've got some extra junk my mom threw in my lunch. You can have some."

The threads that held my life together were coming apart like a pair of jeans whose knees have given out, where the side seams are held in place only by those long white connector threads. I could practically watch it unravelling right in front of my face.

"I think I better return this," I mumbled to Ari's back as we exited the school.

She glanced back, her hair glowing in the sunshine, ready with a comeback for me, but on seeing the look on my face, she didn't argue, but just grabbed my arm and dragged me over to where Deena sat.

"Just wait," she ordered. "Just wait one sec before you redial that missed call. Sit down, have a sandwich . . ."

"No." I flipped my phone open and punched in the return number.

My back was against a tree for support. Deena sat nearby with watchful eyes, while Ari shrugged and opened her lunch bag. She pulled out a wrap filled with sliced vegetables and hummus and started eating. While the phone rang, she held a second wrap out to me and I took it and laid it next to me on the grass, my mouth already watering.

"Hello!" An angry strange voice barked out at me. After grumpily confirming who I was, the owner of the voice sounded if anything even more irate and upset than originally. "Your phone number was on this woman's cellphone as the person to call in an emergency," he growled. "Where the hell are you, anyway? I called over an hour ago! Your mother is here at my house and someone needs to come get her. Her car is parked in my driveway, and she's insisting she lives here. She won't leave!"

"Can you put her on?" I dropped my head in my hands and saw Deena flash a look at Ari. "Please?" I added.

"James?" It was her, all right. "James, it's mommy!"

"Hi Mom."

"James, did we ever get the money from that old teapot? Because this man here says he never saw the silver teapot and I'm sure, I'm absolutely positive, we brought it in here a week ago and he said he'd give us money for it. I want to look for it, but he won't let me."

There was a muffled shout from somewhere at her end and she shushed the other person violently.

"What? What teapot?" This was incredible. It was too weird. And a flash of anger surged up in me. "Mom, where are you? Put that man back on the phone!"

"You know, the old one from my granny. Remember? The one with the carving and the handle. It's so elegant. I'm positive it's worth a fortune, and this man here says he doesn't have it. He's cheating us, James! I won't allow anyone to cheat us!"

"Mom," I tried again, "just put the guy back on the phone, OK? Let me talk to him."

"You want to handle it for me? OK, then, you can be the man in the family," she chortled, "and defend your mommy against this wicked old man, who . . ."

There were the sounds of a brief scuffle as she hollered into the phone something about cash and silver and being robbed, before the male voice came back on.

"Listen, kid," he said, "I have no idea what's going on here, but this mother of yours is driving me crazy. She drove up on my lawn and walked into my kitchen like she owned the place, and that's where she's been all morning. I can't get rid of her. One minute she thinks this is some kind of store and the next minute she's insisting it's her house and she tries to throw me out."

"Can you call her a cab?" I was furiously scrabbling around in my head for ideas on what to do. "Can you put her in a cab? I'll give you our address and she's got money in her purse, so pay the driver up front, OK? Please?"

"What the hell is going on here!" the guy demanded. "What's the matter with her anyway? She crazy or something?"

Possibly, I thought to myself. Very possibly. "No," I said aloud, "no, she's not crazy, just confused. Listen, man, I'm at school and I don't have any wheels or I'd come get her myself. If you give me your address I'll get the car later. Is that OK with you?"

There was a lot of grumbling, and an obvious attempt at grabbing the phone back by my mother, before the guy finally convinced himself he could do these things. I didn't have a clue who he was, but he was upset and probably also a little scared of her if he was anything like me. In the long run, though, he saw the suggestion as a way of getting Mom out of his hair and he agreed, but not before threatening to call the cops.

"No, man, please! No cops. Please. I'll make sure this doesn't happen again." I was begging the guy. "Please. She's just real mixed-up, that's all."

"Well, OK." He couldn't resist digging the blade in a little, which I honestly couldn't blame him for, since in his position I'd have probably done the same. "But this woman is loony, and someone should be looking after her better. She might be dangerous!"

I could hear my mother hooting with laughter in the background while the guy gave me his street address, and while I promised over and over to come get the car out of his way that afternoon.

Ari was chewing away, watching me as I snapped the phone shut after entering the guy's address into contacts. "What's up?" she asked. "Eat your wrap," she ordered, "and you'll feel better. Is it your mom? Is she in some kind of trouble or something?"

I rubbed the heels of my hands over my eyes and took the sandwich Ari was holding out to me. I unwrapped it, and took a bite before answering.

"I don't know," I said with a full mouth. "I honestly have no idea what's going on."

Both girls were watching me, Deena with serious dark eyes and Ari with a bit of a laugh lurking in her face.

"It's not funny," I said. "It's absolutely the furthest thing from being funny."

Ari glanced over at Deena and then said, "Yeah, you're right. I'm sorry. I was just thinking of certain parental oddities I've gone through myself. But that's different and your whole situation is probably not funny at all."

"She's at somebody's house. Some stranger." I was trying to make sense of the whole convoluted story by talking it through. Inside my head the information was all a jumble; maybe if I put words to it, it'd start to make some kind of sense. "She's driving really weird these days, really bad and dangerous, and she's acting odder and odder all the time. Some days she seems to be the same person she always was, and other days it's like she dropped down from another planet or something."

"OK, so she's at somebody's house," Ari said carefully. "So what's the problem? Is she hurt? She didn't hurt anyone else, did she?"

"No, but," and I paused, not even sure where to start. "The guy says she thinks his house is her place, so she tries to kick him out, and then she starts thinking it's a store. A pawnshop actually, because she thinks he owes us money." And as I spoke, memories began to come back, faint at first and blurred around the edges, then sharper.

"Pawnshop?" Deena spoke for the first time.

"Yeah. Y'know, I remember how when I was little we'd head downtown sometimes and she'd always tell me we were 'antiquing,' and made it sound like it was going to be a lot of fun. She'd buy me an ice cream or something for a treat." I shook my head, remembering, grasping at stray fragments of memories that slipped away into wisps of murky scenes and voices as soon as I tried to nail them down.

"And?" Ari was impatient. She wanted the rest of the story, but the problem was the rest of the story was hidden somewhere and I wasn't even sure if it truly was the rest of the story or just something I'd dreamed or made up or saw in a movie.

"I think she pawned stuff to make extra money," I said finally. "I kind of do remember taking some very old silver teapot to a crowded, dirty store downtown. The owner was this really ancient guy with white hair. He reminded me of Santa Claus."

Ari laughed and then I did, too, shaking my head at the memory. "Santa Claus," she mused. "Nice."

"The teapot had a kind of swirly pattern etched into it. Mom had it wrapped up in a towel and she carried it like it was a baby. I remember that part because it was embarrassing, even to a little kid. The thing must have been really old, and I remember the old man gave me his hat to wear, because I was crying and bored and I wasn't supposed to touch anything. His hat was a fedora, like the ones I always wear now, but really old and beat up, just like him. I loved that hat. It was my first one. I wore it until it fell apart."

Mom's latest troubles were forgotten for a few minutes, while memories swelled up inside and I laughed quietly, remembering. "Man, she must have had some good stuff at one point, because we were downtown 'antiquing' a lot in those days. Never do it anymore, though."

I wolfed down the rest of my wrap and Deena held out a cookie to me.

Ari shook her head. "Parents are nuts," she said flatly. "Absolutely whacko. Don't even try making sense of the stuff they do or say because basically they have no idea. They're children inside grown-up bodies."

Deena took an apple out of her bag and bit into it. "Not all of them," she said quietly.

"OK, fine. Not all. But most of them," Ari insisted. She turned to me. "Your mom sounds like she's a little batty, but she's your mom, so what're you gonna do? Where'd she get all that stuff she pawned? Is there more?"

I shrugged. "There isn't anything more. Not as far as I know, anyway. And I don't know where she got the stuff originally. Her grandparents, maybe, or some other relative. We don't have any relatives out here. Mom moved here from Ontario before I was born. The stuff might have come from out there. I honestly have no idea."

"What about your dad? Maybe the stuff was his?"

"My dad left before I was born."

The statement was flat, but it still hurt sometimes to think it. He'd walked away. He'd never even seen me or got in touch later. Never seemed interested enough to find out if Mom or I were still alive.

"I've never met him or his relatives," I continued, "and I've never met any of her family either. It's just Mom and me."

And as I spoke I realized for the first time how absolutely barren that sounded. We were totally on our own. Completely by ourselves, without any kind of backup. It struck me like a solid blow to the gut how single and small and lonely Mom must have felt then, when she was just a young girl not much older than Ari was now, pregnant with me and living by herself waiting to give birth. And how alone she must feel now, when even she must realize in some corner of her messed-up brain that things were definitely going sideways.

It hit me how the things I'd grown up with—our being a family of only two and being on our own for all the birthdays and holidays and never knowing any grandparents or aunts—would have been a huge struggle for her, financially and emotionally, with nobody to talk to or ask a favour of once in a while. How she must have been afraid and apprehensive when she left her birth family all behind, wondering if she could pull it off, re-starting her life here in Alberta.

And then, realizing that her taking on that struggle in the first place, walking that hard path all alone, must have meant whatever happened to her before was so terrible, so hurtful, she needed to completely erase it from her life and begin again.

All of those sensations hit me at once and it felt like a body blow, leaving me almost breathless at the thought of my mom as the young, pretty girl she must have been in those days, worried and lonely, scared and damaged from whatever had happened to her, but brave enough and strong enough to start her life over in a new place.

17

"James? Is that you?"

There was a little tremor in Mom's voice when the screen door bounced shut behind us, and I wondered if bringing Deena and Ari home with me was the brightest idea I'd ever had. It didn't seem so at that point, but at school after the phone call, we'd decided skipping the afternoon, taking a look at Mom to make sure she was OK and then talking Mel into driving us to the stranger's place to pick up the car, was the most workable course of action. Probably all of us figured Mel would be able to talk to the guy reasonably, instead of giving him the chance to go all ballistic with a bunch of teenagers. He'd sounded pretty upset on the phone earlier.

"Mom, what's happening to you?" I was a little unsure of how to approach her. It was impossible to be certain what kind of mood she might be in. "Are you OK? What's going on?"

I hadn't seen her since the morning, and in my mind's eye was a memory of her crying and covered in dripping mascara. Her face was still grey-coloured from the remnants of rubbed-in makeup, but she wasn't crying anymore. One step in the right direction.

The three of us entering the kitchen might have set her back, but she didn't let on. She just waved a casual hand at the girls, both of whom she'd never laid eyes on before, and then turned to me, a look of intense concentration on her face.

"When's Gary supposed to get here?" she demanded. The tremor was gone, and now her tone told me she figured she was back in the driver's seat.

"Gary! Gary who?" Once again, she'd taken me by surprise. I had no idea what she was thinking or where this was going. "Mom," I said, "we need to go get the car. We stopped to make sure you're OK, but then we're gonna phone Deena's aunt and get her to drive us there, OK?"

"Yes, you know. 'Gary'!" she explained with exaggerated patience. "He's bringing over the new tent. You guys are going camping. Don't you remember? You were looking forward to this so much, James, how could you have forgotten?"

Camping? I wondered if she was getting things confused with the winter ski trip I'd had planned to take with Frank and Jen. The one that ended in disaster for all of us.

"Mom," I tried again, "what are you talking about? Who's Gary?"

"G-a-r-y," she said, sounding out each letter. "Gary, your stepdad, you doofus! Honestly!" She turned and laughed at the girls. "He's so forgetful!"

"You mean Gary from way back? The guy who lived with us for a while?" Man, we hadn't mentioned that guy's name since she booted him out, and that was years ago.

"Well, duh," she said and laughed again. "Yes! Yes, Gary. When's he coming back? Is he going to be here for supper, because if he is then I should know." Her voice began dropping into dangerously low territory, the kind of place where recently she had begun crying or screaming from. "It's only fair that I should know. Nobody ever tells me anything!"

"Hey, Mom." I wanted to move her away from any chance at emotional upheaval and get her back on what lately passed for level ground again. "Want to meet Ari and Deena?"

She glanced back at both girls without acknowledging them, possibly not even registering the fact she'd never met them before, and then tossed them a little queenly wave.

It was at that point, seeing Ari and Deena huddled over there in the corner by the entry, obviously uncertain and really quiet, almost invisible, that I was suddenly struck by how miserable the place I lived in must seem to them. The house was in a nice neighbourhood and pretty large by most standards, but its size just meant there was more space to be messed up, more floor for crumbs and dirt to settle on, more counter space to be covered in old toast crusts, fruit peels and crusted pots and pans.

I hadn't noticed the odours before now either, but the kitchen smelled stale and there was a burned and slightly rotten tinge to the air. It was sort of sickening to think Mom and I were living in such a dump, embarrassing to admit I hadn't even seen it happening, and I made a silent vow to clean the place up later—a vow I knew even as I made it I'd probably not carry out very well. Ari started across the filthy floor, aiming an outstretched hand at Mom in order to shake her hand, and I could see the faint disgust registering in her eyes when she stepped on unknown gritty substances underfoot.

"Hi, I'm Ari, Mrs. Campbell," she said, motioning Deena to follow.

Mom just glanced at Ari's open hand in a distracted way. "He hasn't been around lately," she mumbled.

"Mom," I said, focussing in on her again, the house and the girls forgotten for a minute, "who are you talking about? Do you mean Gary, your old boyfriend? You turfed him out years ago."

"Really? Did I?" Her confusion was real. "Why would I do a thing like that?"

My heart felt as if it was literally breaking, and the feeling made me almost nauseous with something like fear. Fear for whatever unknown thing was coming next.

"Yes, Mom, you did. He's gone. Long gone."

"Well," she said huffily, "that's odd. I could have sworn he'd be here for dinner."

"Maybe he will be. In some way. Just not physically, maybe." Ari had found her voice and was, of course, completely off-base as she yanked out a chair and sat down. "And Mrs. Campbell—can I call you Mrs. Campbell?—I'm sure Gary's thinking of you right now, too. Which is why you're thinking of him. Picking up wavelengths in the air. So to speak."

"He is?" Mom seemed entranced by this idea. "You think so?"

"Sure. Why not?" Ari's taste for the absurd was obvious, and she talked as if Mom was really making sense and their conversation was logical. Which it was not. "He might be right around the corner right now, coming on over, thinking about sitting down and having dinner with you."

"That's what I thought!" Mom was triumphant, and glanced at me in a reproving way. "That's exactly what I thought! He knows I'm a good cook."

"Of course he does."

"And Gary is my one true love."

"And true loves never go away," Ari said gently. "They are always a part of you."

Mom's eyes teared up and she spoke with difficulty. "They are, aren't they? I miss him. I miss him dreadfully."

"Well, I'm sure he's thinking about you, and that's why you're thinking about him," Ari said, and if she'd stopped there it might have been OK, but Ari's not one for stopping until someone forces her to, and so she continued. "And you know how people can surprise you. How you're thinking of them one moment and most of the time you can barely remember their names and you wouldn't even recognize them on the *street* and then suddenly they're in your thoughts and a day later or maybe a month later, there they are! Right in front of you!"

Mom looked confused for a second, and then she nodded in a tentative way.

"So probably what's happened," Ari said, "is that this Gary guy is in your thoughts for a reason. Maybe he's in trouble!"

At the sudden look of panic on Mom's face, Ari added quickly, "But probably not. Probably he's not in trouble at all. Maybe he had a piece of really great news! Maybe he caught a big fish or, I dunno, maybe a moose or something."

At my look, she said defensively, "Well, your mom says you guys camp, so it could happen."

"You don't just 'catch' a moose," I said warmly, "like catching a cold or something, and secondly, what the hell are you talking about?"

Deena cleared her throat and spoke up. It was a relief to hear from someone else.

"I'm gonna call Mel," she said, "so she can meet us here and maybe . . ." She trailed off, but I knew what she was trying to say.

The three of us were completely unequipped to deal with Mom's troubled mind. And I was afraid if she blew up again as she had that morning, Ari and Deena might just figure it was better to be out of it all and leave me there alone with her. Which was not a thing I wanted to happen.

Mel's presence proved to be the turning point. As soon as she walked in the back door, everything changed. She put an arm around Mom and led her to sit at the table, ordered Deena to make some tea and asked Ari to take me outside for a little while. It was the three of them in there and the two of us outside, sitting on the porch, not talking. Even Ari didn't seem to know what to say anymore, and believe me, I was grateful for the silence. After the past few days, weeks and months, even, I was beginning to realize how under-rated silence is.

It's hard to see your mom or anyone else you've known since before you can remember as anything other than what you've got accustomed to, but for a second I'd glimpsed what mom must have looked like to Mel. What I saw then was a woman who was more than a bit of a train wreck. Her eyes were reddened and sore looking, her hair was greasy, she hadn't been showering very often lately so she looked grubby and didn't smell very good either, and in her face there was a desperate fear. And at the same time, you could still see the shell of the woman she'd once been—that pretty young blond on the swing with me. That person still lurked behind her hopeless eyes.

And while it felt extremely weird having this near-stranger come over and take control of my crazy mother, it was also a stranger whom I felt a sort of warmth from that had nothing to do with her being Deena's aunt and was rooted instead in her seeming like just a really nice, comfortable and caring person. It felt good and safe having her around.

"James." Mel's voice interrupted my thoughts and Ari and I both stood. "Your mom is going to need to see a doctor."

She came through the back door onto the porch and sat on the railing, facing us. "She's not well, James. She veers in and out of coherence, and that is something she needs to have checked out, but first we'll solve the car issue. Deena will stay here with her while the rest of us go retrieve your mom's car."

And that's how it was handled. It was so easy. After all the strife and the crying and screaming, and me feeling like my head was gonna explode from tension, all it took was someone telling me a simple plan and then helping to carry it out. Done deal. Awesome. Made me think women are underappreciated. Not for long, obviously, but for a couple of hours. Until we brought the car back and the three of them left and I was alone with Mom again.

18

"Who was that?" Mom whispered when Mel and Ari and I brought the car back and the door closed behind them and an obviously relieved Deena. "Who is that woman and what gives her the right to tell me what to do?"

"Mel is Deena's aunt," I started, and I only got that much out before Mom broke in again, her voice rising in pitch.

"Why was she here? I don't like the way she looked at me." Mom pushed her hair behind one ear and a look of intense concentration came over her face. "I bet I know why she was here! I bet she's trying to steal some of our stuff! Our things are nice, the things we have here, and she probably thinks she can steal it and sell it. People like her steal stuff. They can't be trusted. It happens all the time."

And when I shook my head in disbelief, she insisted, "Well, they do! You read about it in the papers all the time."

"Mom, she's trying to help."

"Help who? I don't need any help! I'm fine and I do not want strangers in my house again, James! You keep that woman away from me." Mom gave an exaggerated shiver. "She's evil! What are you and those people doing behind my back?"

"Mom, she's not evil. She wants to help us. She thinks you need to see a doctor, and I think she's right."

"A doctor!" Her reaction wasn't a surprise to me, and all I could do while her voice rose was find a chair and sit down, waiting for a chance to get a word in.

"Is she Indian?" Mom demanded. "Her and that girl she had with her? Not the talkative one, the other one. Why are there two Indians in my house?"

For a second I wondered if she even knew who I was anymore, if she could see me and my brown skin and black hair and dark eyes. It seemed possible she was losing track of who I was and in the process losing herself as well. For the first time, I started to think we were going to need some serious outside help with all this.

"Mom, maybe I need to know about my dad. And some of your relatives."

It was a shot in the dark, but it was desperation time, and at that point I'd do or say just about anything to stop the flow of words coming from her. Words that I knew I'd remember forever and that I wanted to stem before it got to the point where I'd end up spending the rest of my life just trying to forgive her for what she'd said.

"Maybe if I knew a little about my dad and about your parents, maybe I could help you better," I said. I was thinking that maybe if I had some inkling of what my father had been like, maybe I'd understand how emotionally fragile she was and the reason she was so rabidly defensive whenever any hint of him came up.

She was sitting there, opposite me at the kitchen counter. Her mouth drooped open a little as I spoke what for us were unspeakable thoughts. "Do you have parents somewhere who could help us? Or other relatives?"

For once it seemed she was so shocked she was speechless, and I carried on. "Dad was Cree, right? Do you know any of his family? Because maybe they'd know where he is and he could help us."

"Why? Why do you have to know this stuff now? What good is it going to be? You've changed! You're so different!" Her voice was desperate, but at least she wasn't talking all paranoid about Mel and Deena anymore. "What happened to my happy boy?" she cried. "You used to be so carefree and so funny! You and Frankie were so funny!"

"Frank's dead, Mom. Things just aren't that funny anymore."

Her back stiffened, and she drummed her fingers on the counter before speaking.

"I don't know anything about your dad's family," she said finally. "He didn't know anything either, or at least that's what he said at the time. He said he was adopted and he had no family. Who knows? Maybe that was all a lie, too, just like he lied about loving me. Maybe they live around the corner!" She flung a hand out wildly. "Maybe they all know about us and they're laughing at us, and that's why he never came back. I don't know what happened. I don't know where anyone is!"

Her voice broke a little, and before she could get caught up in crying it seemed maybe if I could get her headed in a different direction I'd get some answers from her.

"He loved you, Mom. He did."

I had no real idea of what the man had felt for her, but in reality what he'd honestly felt for her at the time when she and he were together meant nothing anymore, anyway. What counted was now, her feelings now at this moment. And now she needed to believe in something.

"Look," I tried again, "I'm positive he loved you, and you have to believe it too. But it's just that something's going on inside you right now. Something is not quite right, and we have to find out what it is. Maybe a doctor might be able to help. Or maybe a counsellor or something. And if you have a sister or a brother somewhere back where you grew up, maybe they'd be able to help, because this sort of thing might have happened to other people in your family."

"You want to go live with my sister?" she whispered. As usual, she had completely misunderstood my words, and now her dismay was obvious.

"No," I said as patiently as I knew how, "that's not what I meant. I don't want to live with your sister or anyone else in your family. Do you even *have* a sister?"

This was the first inkling I'd had that there was anyone out there related to us, and for a moment I was at a total loss, imagining an aunt, grandparents, maybe cousins, out there somewhere.

"I just want to know if there is anyone back where you grew up," I continued. "Anyone in your family, who might be able to help us. Help *you*. Maybe it's genetic, what's happening inside you, and maybe they can give us some advice."

She barely waited until my words were out before starting off on another riff, slamming a fist onto the counter for emphasis.

"You are mine!" she yelled. "*Mine*! None of them love me. None of them ever cared about me or loved me. None of them matter."

"Mom!" I interrupted, "I don't want to live with any of them! I just want to know if you've got any . . . ."

"And your so-called 'father'!" Here her voice practically failed altogether while she gathered venom. "He didn't do anything but get me pregnant! He never even came to see me after that. I had to go to the hospital all by myself. He never even came to see you. He's a waste!"

She was crying in earnest now, the tears running again over her cheeks, her voice wobbling. "Why do you ask about him? Why? Why do you want to hurt me?"

She leaned there at the counter with her head bent while the sobs took over her body, her shoulders shaking with the power of her tears. The emotions were emptying her, dumping their toxic mess all over our kitchen and fouling the air. She made no effort to clean her face or wipe her eyes. She was lost in her absolute emotional meltdown.

And I was empty. I couldn't feel a thing. I turned and walked to my room. Closed the door. Picked up my guitar and started strumming.

19

The next morning she knocked over the neighbour's garbage cans on her way to work and sent them careening down the street, scattering flying bits of eggshell and unrecognizable crap all over the road. But after that incident, after I went over and smoothed things with the guy and picked up his scattered rubbish, apologized like a madman and promised it'd never happen again, things suddenly grew calm once more.

Everything settled down. For days, and then weeks, I watched her, waiting for a break in her façade, waiting for her to start screaming and crying, but nothing happened. She cooked dinner, she went to work, bought groceries and did the laundry. The house got clean again. All the crap that was pushed into corners and smeared when I tried to sweep or clean the counters disappeared, and the house even smelled good again. She was back to what passed for normal in our household, and I began to relax, figuring maybe she'd been going through some kind of complicated female inner glitch that had somehow sorted itself out, a monthly thing that had grown and expanded for the past year and then gone completely out of whack.

Life was quiet, the screaming stopped and her makeup stayed where she put it, and for all of that I was grateful. She still drank way too much at night, but she was back to being the mother I was familiar with, and I relaxed my guard enough to get a part-time job bagging groceries at the supermarket down the block. Summer vacation loomed in the near future, and I knew I'd be able to work full-time and actually save some money. Working after school and on weekends kept me busy, tired me out, stopped me from thinking too often about Frank, Jen and the dream. It was the respite I needed.

The open mic at Blues Inverted was my second home and as long as I got back to our place on time, Mom seemingly didn't have a clue I was down there. Which in turn meant I could go there without dreading meltdowns later. I could go to Crimson Street, hang out, say hi to Mel, who I actually looked forward now to seeing. I could drink the muddy free coffee while listening to some really good music, then go home and have dinner or go to bed. It was a lonely life in a lot of ways, and there weren't any laughs or bouts of mad-girlfriend nuttiness, so it was boring, but it was calm.

People who've lived through a hurricane describe the eye of it as eerily silent and yet somehow heavy and menacing. In that same sense our life at home felt peaceful, but odd at the same time, with a sort of unseen threat lurking behind us somewhere. Life was quiet though for a change, and that's what I was hanging on to. Maybe I should have recognized it for what it was, a brief pause in the craziness, when the days at home simmered down again, but I didn't. Didn't have a clue. Thought to myself, well finally! Finally we can get back to normal. Which is where I was wrong.

Because one bright summer afternoon, when the sun shone and birds sang and all the world just felt warm and happy, Mom knocked over a light pole on her way home from work and nothing in our lives would ever be the same again.

The light pole incident totalled her car, and the fact that she was moving at a speed completely off the dial and wasn't wearing her seatbelt at the time of impact, meant Mom hit the windshield so hard she cracked it as well as her skull. Her spine was compacted and messed up in places and she broke several ribs. There was internal bruising and bleeding from when her body hit the steering wheel. So, in other words, she was a mess, but she was alive.

All of this in turn meant the paramedics were called to the scene of the accident and she was taken to emergency, where, after waiting in a hallway for what seemed like an eternity and was at least long enough for the emergency workers to call me and for me to find a ride over, she was finally admitted and taken to a bed on the fifth floor of the University Hospital.

And once that happened, once hospitals, doctors and nurses got involved, there was no turning back and no hiding our problems.

After a week of tests and return visits on my part and screaming rages and crying jags on hers, I was worn out. The hospital staff were rambling on about a potential brain tumour, but at the same time not actually sticking with that diagnosis and instead dropping other crazy medical terms as possibilities, but then not sticking with those either, and I was on autopilot. Exhausted by all of it—the fear, the guilt, the foreign smell and noise of the hospital itself with its confused and fear-ridden visitors and its uniformed staff, and the endless, endless talking. It hurt like crazy to see Mom so helpless, like a bug under a microscope, almost ignored by the hospital staff sometimes while they looked, poked, prodded and discussed her with each other as if she were deaf and inanimate.

And I was helpless. Incapable of being honest with her, since I had little or no idea what anyone was talking about, and unable to even act normal around her. A lot of the time the only part of the daily medical discussion I could understand was the part where the doctors were saying they really weren't sure, didn't fully understand what was causing her behaviour, and would have to do more tests.

How was I supposed to interpret that for her? *Hey Mom, you're really unique! One of a kind! Nobody knows what's wrong with you; they just know it's something really bad and you're not getting better anytime soon.* I couldn't do that to her. So instead, I sat and talked about school and told her I was looking after her plants.

Hanging around the hospital was like travelling to a different country where I only spoke a few words. Where maybe I knew how to say 'please' and 'thank you' to the natives, but all the real intricacies of language, all the terminology and slang, were indecipherable. My body felt like I'd never run or ski or goof off ever again. Part of me felt like it was dying.

Mel and the girls gamely did their bit and were still there for me whenever I was desperate enough to call on them, but let's face it, calling what amounted to almost total strangers to come over and help me deal with my mother just seemed too lame, although Mel's familiarity with government regulations and paperwork came in real handy. Got me pointed down that long highway of government health forms and various supporting documentation in order to make sure mom was looked after properly and that I'd be the one doing the looking-after.

I was determined it would be me taking care of her, doing what needed to be done to keep her comfortable and, I hoped, eventually cured of whatever it was she was battling. The fact that I was nearing my 18th birthday meant we could dodge a lot of the types of government interference that might have once led to me being placed into some sort of family-care situation. I was nearly an adult myself, and I made that fact very clear to anyone and everyone. And for anyone who may have missed it, Mel was there to reiterate and strengthen my argument.

But even so, sometimes all of it was more than I could handle without breaking down myself, and when she got completely out of hand, I'd steer Mom gently back into her hospital bed, lavishing her with random promises for whatever she was into at that moment, and then leave her there for the nursing staff to deal with. But I could only be hard-hearted like that on rare occasions. The rest of the time, we struggled, she and I, to find some sort of common language.

It's hard to describe the sense of deep responsibility I felt for her at that time. It was almost like we'd traded positions and she was the kid and I was her parent, that's how potent the sense was of being the one in charge of her well-being. It felt as if her life depended on me, that there were unseen dangers lurking all around us and I needed to protect and nourish her so that she'd not just survive but also thrive and be happy. And that role, me being the parent and thinking of Mom as my child, surprised me by seeming so normal, so realistic and easy, as if she and I had just traded skins for a while like a couple of snakes shedding their old ones for something else.

Her obvious fear that she'd die and be left behind, somehow forgotten and obsolete, was one of the hardest things to reason with. It was tough having to try to convince her over and over again, knowing all the while that my arguments and persuasion were probably going to be futile, that no matter what happened, I'd never desert her like my dad had, never forget her like he did, and always be there for her. And at the same time, I had a life to live myself and meals to eat, tests to take at school, worries about meeting bill payments, and things that she'd handled before and that I now had to tackle on my own.

In the midst of it all, I was positive that deep inside her screwed-up brain she was trying just as hard as I was. That photo from when I was a little kid, of me on a swing and her on the one next to me, was in my room on my dresser to remind me she wasn't always this way, that deep inside her was the Mom she'd once been. It was the only lifeline I had.

20

That summer the days fell into an off-the-radar routine. When I wasn't bagging groceries, I'd be hanging around at the hospital, if Mom was an in-patient at the time, and I'd spend most of my time there encouraging her to swallow some of the hospital food. Sitting next to her, I'd pick bits of her meal off her plate, hold them temptingly in front of her nose, and tease her into swallowing some of it. Most of what was served she scorned as 'slop.' Some of it she'd eat. Some of it, to be honest, if I was hungry enough, I'd eat for her. Between us we got the job done.

She'd gossip about the nurses, and I'd watch the doctors when they made their rounds. I'd listen in as they compared notes, in the vague hope of making sense out of what they were saying. On the days she was recuperating at home, I'd take off as early as possible in order to avoid the home care workers, who, although they were usually friendly, were also in my house, my space, and making themselves comfortable there for their shifts.

More and more often I found myself thinking that my actual home didn't even exist anymore, but that instead I carried a kind of portable home with me wherever I went. It was like morphing into a two-legged, talking, walking tortoise—at home in the space where I was, holed up in my shell, where I could pull myself inside and hide whenever things on the outside got bad.

These home care men and women would roll in with their go-cups, their bagged lunches and their private burdens, and they'd start talking the minute they came through the door. Sometimes it seemed like they were such non-stop communicators they were probably already talking to us during the drive over and just continued the conversation once the back door closed behind them.

It was good they were there, because they took care of the private things with Mom's care, but at the same time it was unnerving to have strangers walk into my kitchen every morning. It gave me a sense of being out of place in the place I should be most at home. Their presence left me feeling unmoored, and it was that sense of disconnect that drove me to Crimson and Blues Inverted nearly every day to walk, listen to music, and hang with people who, no matter how drunk, dysfunctional or weird they might be, at least weren't physically sick or demanding that I do stuff for them.

Then, one August morning, after rushing it to the hospital to sit with her while she tackled her breakfast, I left Mom early and bussed my way downtown to the Metis Community Core Centre.

M-Triple-C was lodged in a scrappy little building in the centre of the city, on a corner lot with graffiti on top of graffiti sprayed all over the benches and the outside walls. A little intimidating, to be honest, considering some of the guys who were smoking around the front door, but I was late for work already and had no time to reconsider my choice.

The woman behind the main desk was about Mom's age—polite, not exactly friendly, but not unfriendly either. Jeans, ponytail and red plaid shirt. Neutral. Her dark eyes slid past me, settling somewhere over my left shoulder, while she handed me the documents and explained what information was needed. She didn't ask any questions or offer any advice, which suited me fine since I'd gone in with no intention of actually talking to anyone. Getting in and then getting out again were as far ahead as I'd allowed myself to think.

So I wrote his name on the sheet of paper, the name that was only a word for me, the name he'd told Mom back when he was in her life. It was a name that in my mind didn't represent any actual body or face, and represented nothing in my heart other than confusion and a sort of semi-darkness, but it was still a name.

'Beland'. Johnny P. Beland. No idea what the 'P.' stands for, or if Johnny was his whole name or a shortened form of Jonathan.

Unlikely to be Jonathan. Probably just 'John.' It sounded like the kind of name the guys who played at Blues Inverted might come up with after one too many barley-pops: 'Johnny Beland and his Blaring Blues Blasters!,' or something equally lame but colourful, and it might not have been his name at all, but it's the one he told her.

If he wasn't the lame-ass jerk I'd always thought he was, and if he happened to be out there somewhere looking for me or for Mom, or if any of his family was looking for us, they'd have a better chance now of finding us. I didn't know where to start searching for them, and for that matter I still wasn't positive I really wanted to find any of them, but this was a beginning of sorts in coming to terms with my father's background and exploring the possible source of some of Mom's emotional hang-ups. I figured maybe her current illness as well, if it was based on stress or depression, might be linked to this Johnny guy. There might be some clue, if I could talk to him, to an aspect of whatever was driving her over the edge now. It was a long shot, I admit, but even a long shot is worth exploring if you're desperate enough.

In my own head it still seemed like all he was in my life was a sperm donor, but a little part of me also couldn't ignore how content and happy Deena seemed to be, living in that little house with her Aunt Mel. And discovering a relative of any sort who might be as willing to accept me and to give a little care to both Mom and me seemed like the sort of goal it was worth putting some time and effort into. My gesture was only a half-step toward my father's family, but that half-step was all I was willing to make.

At the same time, I couldn't shake the thought, or maybe it was a dream, that someday I'd meet someone with that last name who was genuinely glad to meet me.

"That's great!" Ari was totally on board, as I knew she would be, when I confessed, somewhat shamefaced, that I'd been down to the Metis Centre. "That's so awesome! Can I meet them after you meet them? I bet they're really nice! Will you introduce me?"

And once again, while she freaked out all over the place, I wondered why I'd opened my mouth and confided anything to her.

"Listen," I said, interrupting her excited rambling before it had a chance to go out of control on me, "wait a sec, Ari, all I did was go down there. I didn't do anything else. Nobody even talked to me except the one lady who had to look for the paper for me. That's it. Nothing's gonna come of it anyway."

"You don't know that! Maybe your dad's been looking for you for years. Maybe he's a super-nice guy and he just somehow, y'know, somehow . . ." Her voice trailed off and I shook my head at her.

"Yeah, a 'super-nice guy' who left Mom by herself to have me. Yeah. Real nice guy, all right."

"He might've had reasons."

Ari took a huge bite out of her apple and sat back on the steps. We were outside on the little plaza next to the grocery store on my break from bagging, sitting in the sun and trying to forget school was right around the corner again.

"For instance," she continued, "maybe he got a job out of town or something. Far out of town. Like hours and hours away, so he couldn't visit you because his car was a piece of junk. Or he didn't have a car, even. Maybe his family lives somewhere else a long ways away and there was an emergency, and his dad was real sick and stuff, and they insisted he come back and when he went back, maybe he couldn't find a way to come back here. To your mom and you. There could be tons of reasons!"

"Reasons," I mocked. "I'm sure he had great reasons. Ones that lasted for 17 years."

"Or maybe he was hurt or maybe he even died or something. Or"—her eyes grew huge—"maybe he was on his way back to your mom, all sorry and repentant and stuff, and he got hit on the head and forgot his name."

I laughed. "Now you think he's got amnesia? Give me a break!"

"Or was killed in the accident he might have had!" She never stops. "But then you'd never get the chance to meet him and that'd be awful! So instead, maybe he was really badly *hurt* in the accident and his memory came back, but he can't walk or anything, so he's in a wheelchair or he has a fake leg or something and he didn't want to trouble your mom because he felt he'd be just an extra burden and all. Maybe that's what happened."

She leaned back and turned her face to the sun, while I thought about this man who'd helped make me and then dropped out of sight.

"Maybe," I said grudgingly. "He might have decided not to come back for some good reason. Not," I added quickly, "any of those wacky ideas you came up with, but some real reason."

"Like?" She sounded miffed.

"Like he thought he'd be a lousy father and I'd be better off without him," I said quietly.

"Well in my personal experience," she said frostily, "fathers are a lot easier to deal with than mothers, so I would bet you money that something he couldn't control stopped him from coming to find you. Maybe your mom moved and never let him know where she went."

That was a completely believable scenario, but one I'd never considered before, and for a few minutes I was silent while Ari chewed her way through her apple.

"But if that's the case," I said finally, "then he's had almost 18 years to figure out where she went. He's had tons of time to look all over the city for her and besides, even before computers and online maps and stuff, there were telephone books. He could've looked her up and found her number."

"Maybe she changed her name."

I looked at her, sitting there so calm and hungry, devouring her lunch, and just shook my head. "No way."

"Why not?" Ari's consistently persistent if nothing else. "If it were me," she said slowly, working her way through the subject, "and, say I got unexpectedly pregnant. Not that I ever would or anything," she assured me, completely wrapped up in her own imagination. "I'm not that dumb, no offence, but let's just say I did, and I was totally scared and maybe royally pissed at whoever got me pregnant. Maybe I'd do something like that. I'd be so scared, y'know, and really angry, furious!, thinking about all the pain of having a baby, all by myself."

She stopped talking to dig in her lunch bag again, and then continued. " And the money! Think about the cost of diapers alone! Oh, man, and toys and playschool. It'd be totally mind-blowing, and I know for sure I'd be absolutely, completely *pissed* at the guy who ran away. I'd probably figure, you *jerk*, you don't deserve to meet your beautiful baby! You're scum! You're a liar and a coward!"

She was really warming up to her subject and I motioned at her to stop. For once in her life, she paid attention and turned back to her lunch instead of haranguing me further.

"I don't think Mom would change her name," I said finally. "I don't think she has it in her, and anyway, her name now is the same one that's on my birth certificate."

"Well, duh." Ari looked up to the sky as if looking for someone to sympathize with her and shook her head. "Of course she didn't change her name *after* she had you! That would be just stupid!" She smiled at me with a kind and weary sort of look that infuriated me. "You're so naïve," she said sweetly. "So young in so many ways."

"And you're just plain crazy," I answered, stung into retaliation.

"Your mom would have changed her name *before* she had you. She'd have given a fake name at the hospital and then decided to keep it. That's what I'd do! I'd call myself Margaret Von Bligh." She sighed and I groaned, dropping my head in my hands. "Or something aristocratic like that. Something kinda cool. Maybe Brandy Silver, like an old movie star. Mona!" She snapped her fingers and sat straight up. "Mona Something. Mona Scrimshaw!"

"*Mona?*" I shook my head. This conversation was going nowhere. "We don't know she did that." I was frustrated, but still trying to keep my temper under control.

"This is nuts," I said. "All I wanted to do was open a door, just a little bit. I don't intend to actually find him. Maybe an aunt or something, or a cousin, but not him. He means nothing to me."

"Deena found her aunt that way," Ari replied, "but not her dad. I don't think she wants to find her dad, either, so you're probably right, you probably won't actually find him, but maybe you'll find some really neat cousins. Those kind of dads seem to disappear pretty easily. Maybe you've got an uncle or something, though. Deena found Mel by putting her name out there into the Universe, and they make a really cool family together. You might find somebody like that."

It was like she was reading my mind and I didn't like it, all this comparison to Mel and Deena and the tight unit they formed. It wasn't like I was looking for a change in my family group exactly; I was only thinking there might be someone else out there who was related to me and who I might want to meet.

"Look," I said, and by that point I was honestly losing any patience I'd started out with, so my voice probably came out a little harsh, "what worked for Deena is great. It doesn't apply to me. I don't see myself as anything but me. I don't define myself by being Metis. Or by being part-white or anything else!"

I paused and glared at Ari, who was still chowing down. It was incredible how much that girl could devour and still stay so skinny, and somehow her continuing to eat while I talked annoyed me even further. I intended to make my position, which was one I had no intention of debating any further, totally clear to her. "Biologically, everyone's part-something! All that does is tell you their parents were such and such, or their grandparents came from someplace else. It doesn't tell you anything about the real person inside the skin!"

I looked her straight in the eyes. "I don't care," I said slowly, enunciating each word, making sure she saw how intense my meaning was, making sure she couldn't drop eye contact no matter how uncomfortable it became. "I do not care about him. I don't care where he is or what happened to him or how he feels about me. He forfeited any right to anything to do with me when he never came to see me. Ever. He is not my 'dad;' he was my father. He fathered me and that's all he did. End of story."

"Okay. Yup. Point taken." Ari was finally finished eating. She rolled back onto her elbows, face up to the sun, eyes squinting.

"But still," she persisted, "maybe he was a truly awesome cool guy and he's just been misunderstood all this time, and maybe he's got awesome cool parents who would now be your grandparents! And who miss you and always wondered what happened to you. How great would that be? You know," she urged, "grandparents who do sweat lodges and stuff, and raised him to be proud of who he is and would love to meet you, and maybe he braids his hair and he's really into music and art and . . ."

She could have gone on forever and I knew that.

"He's a sperm donor, Ari! He's nothing!"

"Well, why'd you go down there, then?" Her chin was thrust out and her eyes snapped at me. "Why're you always so pissed off anyway? How come you can't just confess to yourself that you're curious?"

"I'm not curious!"

"You are! Or if you're not curious, then you're suspicious, or you're hoping for something you don't have or you're thinking some-one will know something more about your mom and all of her prob-lems and issues and . . ."

"Shut up! You crazy clucking girl-hen!" And I honestly had no idea where that came from or why I was so over-the-top furious with her. She was driving me up the wall with frustration, and the words just boiled out of me. I was enraged to the point of not even caring anymore if I sounded idiotic or made her mad and lost her as a friend. How any one person could be so completely annoying and drive me so insane with rage was beyond my comprehension.

Ari's pointy chin dropped down. "What?" she squeaked. "Clucking what?"

For one long moment she just glared at me, and then she started to laugh. Threw her head back, laughed until the tears came, and then reached over with her long skinny arms and pulled me into a massive hug that sucked the breath right out of me.

"Gotta go," she said, scrambling up. "You're a dope." And she left.

21

I'm a man and that's all I am. I have brown skin, black hair, eyes that even to me look a little tired and haunted, and a crazy mixed-up mother whose life seems like it's gonna get a lot crazier and even more mixed-up before she gets any better. And I am living my own life. I'm a man who will walk through that entire life missing his two best friends and regretting their deaths. I'm a man who intends to make sure my life is worth the living of it. And that's all I am.

Hanging at Inverted listening to music, and working at the store bagging groceries for strangers, are not all I am. Neither is going to school or helping my mother eat her meals at the hospital. Those are things I do and things I feel I should do, and sometimes things I *want* to do, but they aren't the total me. Nobody, including me, knows the total of me, and maybe that's as it should be. Maybe some things should remain a mystery, and we shouldn't understand every little detail about other people or even about ourselves, because that makes life just a little too simple for us. Maybe we're supposed to struggle sometimes.

And one day, making my way down Crimson toward the afternoon jam, watching the faces pass me by, unaffected by any of them and yet touched at the same time by the energy or the sorrow or even the boredom reflected in their random eyes, that sense of the mystery of life that was starting to grow inside me, got stronger. Something happened, which at the time just felt weird, but in fact marked another turning point that I could look back to later and marvel at.

There were two turning points, and the first was when a woman walked past me with her kid in one of those backpack deals that certain backwoods-hiking-type moms use to haul their babies around. The kind of kid-carrier that fits onto a person's shoulders and the kid rides around backward, looking out from behind the mom's head, their little heads bobbing around, eyes taking in all the strangeness around them. There are a lot of young moms hanging out on Crimson, carrying go-cups and yakking their brains out with other young moms. This one was no different, but the kid in her backpack was sure different.

He, at least I think it was a 'he,' since it's hard to tell with little kids because they all look androgynous at the best of times unless they're actually wearing a dress or ruffles or pink or something that sets them up definitely as little girls, so therefore I'm guessing here, but, 'he' was riding along in his mom's backpack, a thatch of thistly brown hair sticking up on top of his head like the top of a little carrot and he was really cute. Normally I'm pretty oblivious to how cute some kid might be, but this one kid grabbed my attention and wouldn't let go. He had a bony little pointy face, not all plump and babyish, more like a little rat than anything else, with that thatch of fuzzy hair on top of his skull. He was looking out at the scenery, sucking on his fist and paying a lot of attention to a dog that went past, when suddenly his eyes clicked on to mine and he would not let go.

His stare sent a spark of jagged energy right up my spine, from my tailbone to the top of my skull. The gaze he connected between us had a concentrated and electric quality to it, and I actually jogged a little to get around some slow-walkers and stay behind this mom and the kid in order to not break the chain he'd started between us.

For a couple of minutes I couldn't figure out where I'd seen that face before, that expression in his eyes, and then it hit me. Those eyes of his, those little pinpricks of blue energy, had a familiar crease between them that jogged something in my memory. He was scowling at me in a thoughtful baby sort of way, as if he were concentrating hard on seeing something in me. The kid was frowning at me in precisely the same way Frank used to back when we were little. There were times when Frank was totally focussed on gauging how annoyed I was and planning his next move accordingly in order to throw me off my feet and get me down on the ground. This kid had exactly the same look.

Frank's stare at those times was a narrowed expression, intense and unblinking. And this unknown little kid, only a few months old, not much more than just a brand-new baby, was giving me the same sort of treatment: staring at me in unblinking concentration. Just seeing that kid made my head spin slightly. A hard lump rose up inside, choking my chest, and a slight dizziness swirled through my vision, giving me a sort of vertigo. He really got to me. Enough to make me stop dead in my tracks, bouncing a little on the balls of my feet when a couple of people bumped into me.

I watched as the kid and his mom disappeared in the crowd around the market. His eyes didn't blink; they were locked on mine, until he was completely out of sight.

And I could not possibly explain or forget the power of that stare he sent to me. It was like a jolt of sheer energy passed between him and me, and I was absolutely sure, more positive than I had been about anything else in my life up to that point, no matter how crazy it might sound, that he was Frank and that Frank had come back. And that thought, that impression, eased something inside of me and replaced it with a sort of sense of being left behind somehow. Of missing Frank even more.

While I was still reeling from that experience and trying to decide what, if anything, it meant, and whether or not I could ever describe the sensation to anyone else or would even *want* to describe it to anyone else, the second crazy intense thing that made up the second turning point occurred.

22

Her name was Lisa, the girl who came into my life later that same day, and she was brown-skinned, like me, and alone, like me. She was sitting at the table next to my regular spot at the corner of the bar when I showed up, all beat and tired from walking. I was still feeling confused and off-centre from the kid incident and from dealing with crazy customers and frustrated clerks at the store all morning. Some of the annoyance from work still clung to me like film on my skin, along with confusion and a sort of crazy hopefulness left over from seeing that kid. I was a wreck.

It was a fantastic, hot, late-summer day, the jumpy energy from encountering that little kid was still pulsing around inside me, and for once I had no place else I had to be. Mom was back in hospital undergoing tests again, so there was nobody at home watching every move I made. The sense of freedom, like a huge burden had been lifted, was energizing, and I'd walked all the way to Crimson Street feeling as if the past few months were finally coming into focus instead of being the heaving dark cloud of sorrow I'd become accustomed to lugging around with me.

"Hey," she said, when I hoisted my exhausted self up onto the one remaining bar stool. She had an iced tea in front of her, the glass sweating from the contrast between the cold liquid and the built-up heat inside the bar. She dodged her head around, trying to meet my eyes, until I finally gave in and glanced down at her. "I'm Lisa."

"Yeah, hey yourself." Rude, I know, but honestly I had no interest in talking to anyone. All I wanted was to sit, zone out, listen to the band, and let the afternoon's events soak in.

"So." She paused and smiled a wide-mouthed beam at me. "I've never been here before. Very cool, this place."

With the amount of time I'd spent down at Inverted, not very many of the characters who hung out there were complete strangers to me anymore, but I knew I'd never seen this girl before. Long dark hair swirled in a lazy curtain around her face and over her shoulders. She had big chocolate-brown eyes and a smile that curved up wide, bright and generous. She was the kind of girl a guy would remember, whether he was interested or not.

And she wasn't shy about starting a conversation even when I was less than interested in talking to her, but despite how cute she was I couldn't let myself get started on the whole talking to a girl and flirting part of things. A huge part of me still mourned the loss of Jen, and I figured it always would. Jen had been my first real girlfriend, and there was no way of ever knowing what our lives together would have become if we'd had the chance to grow up together. That question would haunt me the rest of my life. It'd be one of those unhealed scars we all carry. Which is why I was completely unready to move into any territory that might even remotely smack of romance.

The whole girlfriend idea, which, to be honest, had come into my head a few desperate times since Jen's death, made me antsy. I knew I wasn't ready for anything that might turn romantic. Not yet. Ari and Deena were around a lot, and I could hang with them without any worries about possible romance and talk to either of them without any sense of guilt. Being with the two of them was like being around a couple of cousins or droids or something. They didn't feel like real girls to me. They didn't even feel like real friends. What they felt like was people who were related somehow, but not necessarily relatives I'd be that thrilled about having around all the time. Girl cousins or nutty half-sisters or something along those lines—definitely not anything sexual.

Lisa was different, though. She was absolutely a real girl—a beautiful, confident and happy girl, and it kind of threw me for a while. It was the happy part that drew me in—her big, wide vee-shaped smile. There hadn't been a lot of that going around lately.

"Want to see?" She tapped her forefinger hard on my arm and pointed down. On her table was a sketchpad, and she held it out temptingly. "Want to see what I'm doing?"

I shrugged, and she took that slight sign of interest as encouragement.

"OK, so I bought this set of pencils," she started. She waved a small package of what looked to me like ordinary pencils. "They cost a fortune and they're really special pencils, so OK, even though I hate to waste money, I decided to go for the really good stuff and spend as much as I had to spend. Because I want to draw. I've decided to become an artist." Her grin split her cheeks. "Except I can't draw!"

She laughed, and with what seemed a touch of embarrassment opened the sketchpad to the first page, where she'd attempted an outline of the stage and the instruments sitting on it. It was pretty bad. The only way I recognized the stage was because she'd titled the drawing in huge winding letters at the bottom. The next page, when she flipped to it, was even worse. The drawing was supposed to represent the bartender, a guy named Dean, but it really had little resemblance to the actual guy, or to any living being for that matter. And the glasses on the bar, the bottles and spigots, were all lopsided and screwy.

"I know!" She laughed at the look on my face and snapped the portfolio shut. "I absolutely stink at it. But honestly, I want to learn to draw."

When I was still silent, she added quietly, "Someday."

"Someday," I echoed, and found a smile on my own face.

There was something in her complete unconcern about whether I laughed at her drawings or not, that made me want to know more about her. She hit me hard, even on that first afternoon. It didn't seem to matter to her how I felt or what I thought; she was ready to talk to someone, and she made it obvious it wasn't my rugged good looks or sparkling intellect that made her want to start a conversation with me. It was the mere fact that on that first afternoon, I was the person who was nearest.

"You still in school?" she asked, sitting back and scrutinizing me with one eye scrunched like someone assessing an interesting insect. At my nod she said, "Living at home still?"

"My mom's a single parent, so it's just her and me, and yeah, I'm still living at home," I replied. "How about you?"

"Roommate," she answered. "Just a guy I used to hang out with, but he lets me stay at his place. You and your mom get along OK?"

I shrugged, and glanced quickly behind me to make sure Dean was out of earshot. "She's not feeling very good these days. Sick a lot of the time."

The music was starting, the band warming up with a few jokes and off-colour remarks about each other's playing abilities, and Lisa took a long look around at the rest of the clientele, watching as a few of the keeners started finding spots on the floor near the speakers.

"Don't know about you," she turned back and grinned, "but this place is a really crazy mix, and I like it. Being a purebred 'Cree-kanian' myself," she added, "it looks like half my unknown relatives might be hanging out here."

And when I looked confused, she went on to explain that her mother was Aboriginal, and her father, a man she referred to as 'the guy that sired me,' was of Ukrainian descent.

"Never met him," she said, running a forefinger down the damp sides of her glass, "but I'm sure he was just a *wonder*ful guy." There was no mistaking the sarcasm in her voice. "And, she told me a lot of stories about him, so in a way I guess I have met him."

Sipping at her drink, she described how he had been extremely proud of his heritage. She remembered stories her mother had told her when she was little, stories she'd guarded, and repeated to herself, and kept close to her heart, holding them like a hand of winning cards in some game, while working her way through her life without him.

"My mother," she hollered above the music, " always bragged that my dad was really proud of who he was. Proud of his background. He insisted God was Ukrainian, and only understood prayers spoken in Ukrainian." She stopped talking and laughed at my expression.

"Seriously!" she continued. "He liked everything from the old country. He made mom learn to make homemade perogies just like his mother and his grandma once did. Mom said he treated cooking like it was a solemn duty."

Lisa shook her head and looked up at me from under a sweep of hair. "It's what real women do," she said teasingly, "they cook for their men." And she laughed aloud when I pulled her up to dance. "They cook, they clean, the men go outside and work hard. You know how it goes!"

Lisa's description left me with a mental image of women in an assembly line of grannies and aunts, making dough, rolling it out, cooking up potatoes for the filling. Listening to her describe her mother's efforts in the kitchen was actually making my mouth water. The thought of grated cheese, sour cream and bacon bits was enticing, and I think Lisa sensed it because she leaned across the dance floor and whispered in my ear.

"Mmmm," she growled in a throatily seductive voice, "all that work in the kitchen and two seconds on the plate. Reminds me of something else." And then she laughed again at my expression.

We talked before, during and after the first set, yelling at each other over the music and, even getting up to dance a couple of rounds again when the harp player on stage made the place rock so bad we couldn't resist.

Even though she was evidently real little at the time her mom told her this stuff, Lisa still remembered the perogy stories, still remembered her mom telling her how Lisa's father would sometimes become so emotionally overwrought he'd cry while he ate, and while she spoke I envisioned huge salty tears rolling slowly down through the bristles of rugged, unshaven cheeks onto a plate of perogies.

The sight of a big strong, muscular man eating her cooking and crying like a baby was evidently more raw emotion than Lisa's gentle and naïve mother could take. The demonstration of his incredible sensitivity convinced her this man was as strong, compassionate and big-hearted as he was a sobbing wreck. A little boy inside a big man's body. The kind of man she would be happy to call the father of her child. The kind of man she would gladly toil through her life beside.

His manly pride took a fast left-turn into manly arrogance as well, a tendency that, in her infatuated state, she ignored or neglected to see. In his macho pride he'd ended things by leaving her mother hugely pregnant with Lisa while he left the city, theoretically to find a better job. Even though he'd promised he'd make lots of money up north in the oilfields and come back for Lisa's mother, as far as Lisa knew her mother had never seen him again and the belief was he'd found somebody else up there in that city of immigrants who already knew how to make perogies and didn't need to be taught.

"But of course," Lisa continued, "there's no way of knowing what happened to him. He disappeared into the tar sands. Maybe he's still there, eating at someone else's table. Chowing down and crying at the same time!"

Lisa laughed while she talked of her mom, taking the sting out of her history, but the stories she remembered her mother telling all seemed to have happened years earlier; none of them appeared to be recent. There was a kind of frantic glint on her face while she talked, a sort of desperate sound in her laughter, almost as if she was trying to salvage something from the telling of them.

"Hey, want to see some pictures of the man in my life now?"

We were sitting again, our backs to the bar, facing the band while the guys on stage stopped to confer about their next tune. The place was humming with activity, people talking, visiting, getting to know each other, and Lisa and I were only two nondescript actors in this little theatre.

"Here. What do you think of him?" She held out her cell and clicked on the photo album. The last thing I wanted at this point was to be looking at a photo of some big tough boyfriend, but I glanced down anyway. On the screen was a huge black snout, large floppy ears and a tongue that hung halfway to the dog's knees. It was the largest, hairiest animal you could have and still call it a dog.

"His name's 'Thor,'" she said, and flipped forward to another shot. "He's such a great dog. He's probably the best friend I've had in, basically, forever."

That one statement, that little pause before the word forever, stuck in my head and shot into my heart with an aching loneliness.

"What about your mom?" I asked. "Where's she live?"

Lisa took a moment to scan through some more shots of the dog and then right before the music started up again, she flipped her phone shut and said quietly, "I don't know where she is anymore. Jail, maybe."

She pulled an old creased snapshot from her wallet, a photo of her mother taken back when Lisa was a baby. When I asked, she said she didn't have pictures of her father. Taking a long second look, Lisa folded the snapshot gently and inserted it back where it came from.

"I was raised here in the city," she said, "and mom sort of came and went." It was fairly obvious that open as she was about her past, eager as she was to share, at this point she wasn't interested in talking further. "C'mon, let's get out there and show these guys how a real dance gets done!"

Later, while the band took a break and I helped behind the bar, washing glasses, Lisa talked more about being born and raised on what she called the 'Oil City 97th Street Reservation'. She was referring to a stretch of downtown home to mostly the homeless and destitute, a lot of whom are Aboriginal. And she made Dean and me laugh, too, even if some of her stories were more than a little sad and disturbing, and even though I realized she was only sharing the things she felt like sharing. I learned more about her in that first afternoon than I'd learned about most people in my life after months of listening to them talk.

One thing she didn't talk about was the people who'd raised her, except to say she'd had a taste of every sort of foster family in existence.

"It made for lots of variety," she said brightly. "I could write a book."

It was pretty hard to know how to respond to a lot of the stuff she talked about. And even though, after hanging with Ari for any length of time, I was getting used to talkative women, I couldn't help but wonder what was in it for her? How come she felt so comfortable, and was so insistent about talking to me?

"Always wanted a brother," she answered, when I mumbled something about her honesty. "A big brother. Always wanted someone else to share things with."

Dean handed her another glass of iced tea and she looked at me over the rim as she took a sip. "Don't worry," she said, "I know you're not related. I'm not gonna go all sistah-crazy on you."

"Hey, I'm not worried," I answered. "Not worried at all."

And it was true; I wasn't worried. Everyone needs somebody to talk to once in a while, and if I was that person for her, then that was cool. I could handle it. There was no doubt she had things she kept hidden, memories she smothered, but still she was attacking her life with an enthusiasm I could only stand back and admire.

As the summer worked its way into autumn and winter, and the days grew colder and shorter, Lisa ended up, along with me and several other regulars, spending most of her spare afternoons and evenings hanging around at Inverted. Knowing her, talking sometimes, but mostly listening, gave me an impression that life would somehow once again return to spinning along on a dependable axis.

Even though I realized at the time how my friendship with Lisa was one-sided, with her doing most of the communicating, and me being a listening post for her to bounce ideas off, just being useful to someone else who was unconnected to my own past and my own history gave a solid feel to my life. It was a time when most other aspects of my days were obscure or threatening or sad, and Lisa's presence was like an anchor of sorts. We didn't see each other often; she wasn't always at Inverted when I was there, but when she was it was good to dance and talk. Her being there or not being there let me get used to the idea that people will come and go all through my life and that I'll be OK with it, I'll survive it.

Lisa made herself useful once in a while at the bar, she listened with an open mind to whomever was on stage at the time, and she spent a lot of time killing time, as we all did. Until the day she disappeared, leaving behind a sort of ghost of a person I remember and still miss sometimes.

23

Meeting Lisa happened at a time when closing my eyes and collapsing into dreams was a more godawful fate than keeping my eyes open and living with the day-to-day reality of grief and anger. That inability to sleep also meant I was tired all the time, and not just tired in an everyday, yawning during class kind of way, but absolutely dog-tired. Completely dead, like a crazed mutt who's been chasing squirrels all day. So exhausted I could hardly shovel food into my mouth. So worn out my guts felt heavy like lead in the bottom of my belly all day.

But at the same time, not so completely bushed that I stayed home and tried to catch up on sleep. Instead I hung at Blues Inverted pretty much day and night until the manager there started treating me like an unofficial employee. He began having me run around posting upcoming show ads on the door and cleaning up after the various bands had left the stage, rolling up cords and making sure the mics and other bar-owned stuff were locked well away from the sketchier elements the place attracted. He even slipped me a few bucks once in a while.

'Sketchy' is a more diplomatic way of describing the type of clientele the place mostly attracts. Even though the music is nearly always really good, the building itself is such a derelict wreck, with a lousy rep as a low-end seedy bar, it's only the more colourful or brave element of music-lover who hangs out there. It's a place a lot of people avoid, and the creepy characters that stand around smoking outside the entrance and bumming change off anyone who passes by aren't helping the rep any.

One of the music teachers at school was a total non-fan of the place. He's got this crazy ambition that seems to dominate his existence, to convince me and the rest of the people in class that jazz is the only real music around. He's convinced that blues is such a minor form of entertainment it appeals only to a species of low-class mouth-breathers. It's an opinion I disagree with.

An old bald guy who dresses like his wife picks out his clothes for him, he comes in to the school and jams with the keeners, and he's always building up the local jazz venue, Red Dog Sax, as the place to go if you want to listen to 'real' music and be all cutting-edge cool. Only at a true jazz club, he maintains, can one really hear experimental music that plumbs the depths of human emotions. Not my thing, man. Too cerebral, maybe, or just maybe too hard to listen to. In my opinion, he's full of bull and simply too terrified to set foot inside a blues club. Blues, on the other hand, is accessible, focussing as it does on having a lousy day in a lousy life.

The blues kicks ass, man. It's music that digs fearlessly into the kind of wild experience I had no real inkling about: murderous men, manipulative beautiful women, and dark downtown streets wet with a threatening kind of rain. Mossy overhung trees, gators, booze, sweat, tears and heat.

And it attracts interesting people, ones who sometimes felt like a second family to me. It was a window into lives I'd never even dreamed existed. Lives my mother had no doubt hoped I'd never learn about, but they were being lived by people who weren't that different from her or from me, either. These people looked a lot different and sometimes they acted different, but they were still just as vulnerable and full of fear as the rest of us. And they were colourful.

No matter who else dropped by for the music, there were always several groups of heavy old ladies—Aboriginal, white, every colour in between, haunting the place, laughing too loud, and sharing stories. They poured themselves into too-tight jeans and too-low tops, and spent their time sipping at draft beer and checking out the male clientele. The women at Inverted carry their sagging rolls of skin with a certain swagger, not allowing the extra weight around their waist to slow them down. They seem to live comfortably inside their bodies, as an emblem marking years of successful living—a badge, not necessarily of honour, but at least of surviving.

And there's also the occasional truly attractive woman who finds herself there for the music and dancing. Somebody who dresses cool, can dance without looking like she's having some sort of fit, and doesn't over-drink herself into stupidity. But those women are generally less interesting to watch.

Along with the women come bikers in bandanas, a lot of them with long grey hair hanging down their backs, leather jackets and biker chaps, stomping through the place in big, heavy biker boots. They nearly always sport beer bellies that almost defy gravity, that are so huge you expect them to drop off the guys' belts onto the floor. These guys walk with a swagger they've been perfecting for 60 years. Some of them are really old. Probably retired bankers living out teenage dreams.

And most of the time the clientele are pretty reasonable, if colourful, and they provide enough entertainment to more than compensate for the cover charge, even if you're not that interested in the music or dancing. Most of them. There are a few, the ones the bouncers try to catch and turf out before they cause trouble, who are less colourful and more threatening. Usually I don't even see them before the bouncers toss them, but sometimes they scurry through the place before anyone catches sight of them.

"Hey man." It was a new guy, someone I hadn't seen before and he was younger than most of the regulars, probably in his late 20s. I wasn't even sure it was me he was talking to, until he pointed a skinny wavering forefinger at me. "C'mere."

He spoke in a drawl, almost Valley Girl style, with a nasal twist to his voice, and evasive eyes that darted all over the place, but never actually focussed on my face. He wore an expensive artsy T-shirt and jeans that were torn and bleached, and cost several hundred bucks. Not the cheap workingman kind of clothes the bikers and most of the other guys at Inverted wear.

"Why?" I had to holler to be heard, figuring he wanted to place a drink order, and prepared to tell him to go up to the bar himself. The band was doing soundcheck and hitting a lot of pretty sour screams while they were at it. "Whaddya need?"

The guy twisted his backpack around so instead of riding on his shoulders, it sat in front of his chest. His hands were buried deep inside the thing, scrabbling around in a search for something, while his eyes finally lit on mine and bore down for a second before flitting off again.

"Wanna show you something," he said.

"Hey!" It was one of the waitresses, Wendy, a middle-aged woman who wears her bright blond hair spiked into a feathery crown. Her short skirt was canary yellow, riding high up on fleshy thighs, and her blouse tumbled down in a ruffled vee, exposing a mound of freckled cleavage—her 'tip-insurance,' as she calls it.

"Hey, get lost," she snarled at the guy.

His bleary blue eyes stared back at her and he stood there, hands still deep in his backpack, weaving slightly.

Marvin, one of the old regulars who's always sitting near the stage since his hearing's pretty well shot, noticed the commotion and got up stiffly off his chair, his arthritic hips slowing him down while he stretched the kinks out of his bowed knees. He took a few steps toward Wendy and me and motioned at the backpack guy.

"Get lost!" he barked, standing there a little unevenly, his knotted old hands hanging in fists at his side. "Listen to the lady!"

Backpack-boy obviously realized he was in a losing battle. A couple more old biker dudes were looking his way now and the bouncer at the door to the ladies' room was heaving himself off the back wall. The guy took his hands out of his backpack and held them out for us to view.

"Nothin'!" he hollered at Wendy. "I'm not doin' nothin' wrong."

"Fine. Then scat," she said coldly. Her tray was full of pints of draft and she held it on one shoulder, giving the impression she'd just as soon heave it at his head as serve her tables. "I said, 'scat.'"

As he turned and wandered off and the rest of the posse sat back down, she gave me a sideways glance and lifted a couple of her glasses down, placing them in front of the people at the next table.

"Don't hang with that guy," she said shortly, her back to me.

"I wasn't," I started, but she kept going, talking over my voice but still not looking directly at me, almost as if she were embarrassed about something.

"He's bad news," she said, her voice rising above the guitar riffs coming from the stage, "and I know it's none of my business, but if you want to get into the stuff he's selling, don't do it here. The manager won't stand for it. He's been run out of here before for selling."

"I don't want it," I said, and as she stared back at me through the din, I hollered loud enough for her to hear, "I don't want any of it. That's not my thing."

One thing I'd learned from living with Mom and that was there's no way I go anywhere near any kind of booze or drugs; watching Mom deal with both her booze and her prescription drug issues was enough to keep me clear of any of that. One of us had to have their brains together, so I'd always had a built-in reason to refuse it whenever anyone started passing a joint or bottle of rye around, and now was no exception.

"OK, then." She waved a friendly finger at me. "I'm not your mother, y'know, but keep it clean, OK?"

"No problem."

"OK, then," she repeated. She looked at me for a second longer, and then grinned a little shyly. The gold stud piercing in her cheek caught the light and glimmered like a dimple. "Just keepin' an eye on you, that's all," she said. "Just pay attention and steer clear of them guys. Got it?"

She left then, on to another table, more orders, more empties.

It wasn't like she shouldn't worry; it just didn't tempt me. I'd had a few beers hanging at Frank's when his folks were out, and I could see where booze could soften things for a guy. I could see how Mom needed the edge taken off her life and how the booze and smokes did that for her, and seeing it, I knew I didn't want it for me. The edge was the only thing that made me feel alive; I didn't want to blunt it. The sharp edge of pain, the anger and blame, it was all I had left to tie me to them. Wherever they might be.

And then somebody's grandma, a woman with short dark hair, in a cutaway black T-shirt wandered over to stand at my side. Bright pink bra straps showed at the neckline of her belly-baring T, the ragged bottom exposing a browned, chubby midriff. She grinned a gap-toothed, slightly wobbling smile at me.

"Dance, eh?" she said.

The band was just getting started. The Reverend Billy Brown and His Chocolate Choir Boys. Who could resist? And so I left Wendy serving her tables and went out on the dance floor with somebody's grandma and let my feet do the talking for me.

24

But it was Lisa who kept me coming back to Inverted all through the fall. Lisa, whom I looked forward to seeing, talking to, and mostly listening to. We didn't do anything but meet at Inverted and talk. We never tied ourselves down to meeting at certain times or days; our only unspoken agreement was we'd meet on the same side of the bar. Sometimes she was there, sometimes not; it was always hit or miss.

We didn't touch each other except when we danced. There was no talk of me meeting her friends or of her meeting mine or of hanging around together somewhere else. Together we watched the random characters that found their way to Inverted, and made up wild and uninformed guesses about their backgrounds and histories. She talked a lot about her dog, and repeated some of the stories she remembered from her mom, but just through being together like that she became someone I felt a connection to. When she left it felt as if her absence had cut one more thread that connected me to life. It made me see the aloneness of it all more strongly than ever. That no matter how many people we surround ourselves with, we're all alone in this game. And all connected in some weird way at the same time.

I'd struggled through the beginnings of winter snowfall in November and then through the holidays in December, reliving, almost against my will, the way Frank and I used to high-five the arrival of new snow and the start of ski season. At this point last year, we'd been planning our Jasper ski trip. Figuring out foods, transportation concerns and getting parental permission had taken up most of our spare time. Those memories, and the knowledge that skiing with Frank was completely over now, that he was so gone he was reduced to nothing more than a wisp of memory, was something I shared sometimes with Ari. Never with Lisa.

Lisa was a bright spot in my life, separate from most of the rest of it. She knew I had a sick mother and a part-time job, but she knew nothing about Frank and Jen, or even Ari. It was one way of keeping part of my life on a more normal track. I couldn't be the victim, the poor-me guy wandering alone in the world with ghosts around me all of the time. Some of the time, around Lisa at least, I could be a regular guy.

But after that January I never saw her again. She disappeared, and although I can feel a part of her still clinging to me, like fuzz on a wool sweater, and there's a little bit of her energy and her outlook on life still stuck to me, I miss her actually being there.

She was cute and funny, and she took my mind off what was happening at home, where dealing with Mom and her injuries and illness, her recurring hospital stays and even worse, the times when she was at home with me and a parade of home care workers looking after her, were taking all the control I could dig up. And she took my mind off thinking about Jen and Frank and how they were missing their final year of high school, planning for jobs and college, and all the extra stuff that goes along with graduating. They would have been finally seeing a way of getting out of their parents' houses. We would have been thinking about sharing an apartment, maybe, or signing up for some of the same classes at university.

It never occurred to me to wonder if Lisa was doing her last year of high school, too. Never occurred to me to wonder whom she lived with and what she did when she wasn't at Inverted. Somehow I'd just assumed she lived and probably worked somewhere downtown and the fact I knew she was Aboriginal was what led me to believe she had some kind of secret life going on that she wouldn't want to share with me.

Stupid. It was so stupid. And I see that now, but my only excuse is that at the time Lisa and I met I was still so tangled up in regret and blame about the avalanche and my part in it, I couldn't even focus on anyone else. Not really. Which is one more thing I can blame myself for and kick myself around about for the rest of my life. It's gonna be busy during this lame life of mine, poking a blaming finger at my own self all through my days on this earth. Yelling at myself in my head about my stupid inadequacies and my dumb pointless self-blame.

The only way I knew how to deal with any of it was by walking past it all, by not trying to put feelings into words, by allowing music to talk instead of me talking. And I did that through sitting in with the house band, when the guys would let me, when things were slow in the place or one of the boys hadn't shown up. There was one guy in particular who had a talent for talking when he should've been listening, and then ending up incapacitated for a few days at home or in jail, so he ended up being one of my favourite people in the place since his difficulties became opportunities for me.

He'd be slated to play and not show, and that's when I'd see the house band guys start to look around despairingly and then settle on me where I sat in my corner of the bar. They'd shrug and glance around at each other a couple of times, then motion for me to come on up. They'd grab an abandoned instrument from backstage where the cords were kept, and toss me into the mix. Every time he missed a gig, I'd pick it up for him. It even earned me a few extra bucks. I'd play a straight bass line for them, just to keep the rhythm going. Pretty good, too. Not great or anything, not something a music agent from the big city would hear and holler 'sign that guy up!' but I could hold my own, learning to ad lib, learning to read the signs. Spotting that musical dervish, the guy who decides to totally go ape and start blowing on the strings of his guitar, or playing drums with his feet or whatever. Learning to be and let be.

It was a freezing blustery day in January the last time I saw her. Lisa showed up late and uncommunicative. The days at that point were at their shortest as well as their coldest, and it had been dark outside for hours when she finally arrived. The snow blew past the doors whenever anyone opened them up and the band was already climbing up on the stage for their second set, wandering through their equipment and yelling insults back at some of the rowdier element in the place.

I was sitting at the bar watching Dean fill jugs of draft, when Lisa finally blew in. She was huddled into a huge parka, her face pale and a little bruised-looking from the cold. She had her fur-trimmed hood pulled up over a wool cap that covered most of her face, and the shadows they cast highlighted the deep grey circles under her eyes. She looked loaded down with pain and exhaustion. Winter can be hard to struggle through sometimes, and I wasn't sure where she lived or even if she had a warm place to stay, since as part of our unspoken non-interference pact we'd never talked about anything that smacked of current personal issues. She stamped her feet over at the door to knock the snow off and get the blood moving through them. Without a word to either Dean or me, she headed past us to the corner of the bar behind me, leaned against the wall and pulled off her wool hat, her black hair blooming out in a static halo around her head.

She'd cut off all her long waving dark hair, leaving it in a shorn jagged cut topped by thick, shiny bangs with her big dark eyes peering out from under them. It made her look 10 years younger, like a little lost girl. Her eyes, usually warm and full of humour, were now sad, dark things like scared little animals behind that shield of heavy hair. She either wouldn't or couldn't meet my eyes or return a smile. Dean handed her a Coke and Lisa stood there, tapping one foot in time with the music, her head down, sipping at her drink, and showing a serious case of avoidance where I was concerned.

I tried, and in my memory it seems I tried really hard, but sometimes I wonder now if that's honestly the case, or just something I dreamed up to make myself feel better. But I did try to talk to her. Asked her what was up, how she was doing. Told her I liked her haircut. That it looked good on her.

And then she pushed herself away from the wall and ran through the back door out into the alley, and even though I jumped down from where I sat, and went out after her and yelled her name, she was gone. She'd disappeared as completely as if she'd never existed in the first place. On that one day in January, she was there, just like before, and the next she wasn't. Even though I asked for weeks about her, nobody seemed to know where she went or why. And I haven't seen her since, but that doesn't mean she isn't still a part of my life. She is definitely still a strong part of my life. A part I'm hanging on to and not letting go of.

And when she left, I started to realize again how much each one person is bigger and somehow more than just that single 'one,' and how even if they're not right in front of your eyes, or even on earth now as we know it, and as we knew them, they still matter. They still are. They never really leave. They're never really gone.

Sitting there one night, in the dark thinking about it all, thinking about Frank, Jen, and Lisa and how I wanted to be able to do more than just feel them around me, and how I wanted to actually talk to them, I decided to follow up on what Ari'd told me months earlier, about allowing the entities or the ghosts or whatever you want to call them, to stick around and not chase them off. I called her, yelling into my cell over the sounds of the bar, the glasses clinking, voices rising and falling, telling Ari I'd decided. I'd finally decided I want them there. I wanted them hanging around.

"Suh-weet!!" she chirped. "That's totally awesome! Where are you, anyway?"

And when I told her I was at Inverted, she didn't say anything back for a minute or two. Then she hollered to be heard over the bar noise, "Cool! It'll be fun! You'll like it, you'll see!"

And I groaned. Fun is what I knew it wouldn't be. Ever. But maybe it'd be enlightening. Or something. One could only hope.

Lisa was one more person in my life who came into it, made a mark on it and then left a hole behind when they disappeared. It took me a while to realize, but these holes people leave behind aren't empty. They've got walls and a floor and in some ways they are more vibrant than the rest of ordinary life and full of a sort of barely-there energy. In some ways these vacant spots in my life feel more alive than me.

Hanging with Lisa was the first strong hint I had that I could and would survive the events of the past few months, and that I wouldn't be just a wanderer in my barren life forever. She'd brought the first indication to me that my life would one day return to normal and that my grief and regret about Frank and Jen would subside and become a part of me instead of ruling everything I did, and that my fears for Mom would somehow reconcile themselves and allow me to carve out a normal life for myself. Somewhere I'd be able to live and maybe even find happiness again.

25

Life keeps going on. Doesn't seem to matter what you do or how awful things get or how you sometimes wish it'd all just stop for a while. Just stop long enough to let a guy catch his breath. Life doesn't, though. It keeps on going. People around you keep on living their lives, no matter how lousy their lives are, no matter how boring or destructive or just plain ugly, or even sometimes, how nice and sweet and simple. Things still keep ticking over. There's no way of stopping it.

Frank's dad called one spring day, asking me to meet him for a coffee at the local Tim Hortons. It was April, over a year since the avalanche, about three months since I'd seen Lisa. Time was healing things just like they say it does, and when he called it seemed like a good idea to go see the man, although it's quite possible my main motive was to simply get out of the house for a while. Mom was resting at home again after her latest round of chemical-induced healing, and I knew she wouldn't even notice me being gone. She was slumped in her chair in the living room, weak and sleepy from the meds, her current home care assistant hovering, so I left her there in good hands, my homework on my desk, computer running a de-frag.

I hadn't seen either of Frank's parents since the funerals, and idly I wondered if I'd even recognize the guy anymore. There was a little part of me thinking he might be wanting to play 'dad' to me, now that Frank was gone, and I was wondering about how to tell him I had dads enough in my life. There'd been the guy mom turfed out, Gary, who'd probably been the closest thing I'd had to a dad, but now with the various characters at Inverted who seemed to think they were looking out for the young guy, I sometimes felt I had enough testosterone around me to gag a mule.

"Hope you like coffee." Frank's dad was sitting near the window, a large double-double in front of him   and one for me on the other side of the table.

"Sure, I do," I said, wrapping my fingers around the warmth of the cup. "Thanks."

"How've you been? Since the accident, I mean." The man was obviously uncomfortable. Maybe seeing me again, minus Frank, was tough for him. Although that was only a guess, since seeing him, minus Frank, was tough for me.

"I'm OK."

"Been meaning to check in on you," he said and then shrugged, his eyes focussed on something outside. "You know how it goes."

"Yeah."

"Just never got around to it, I guess."

It didn't seem fair he should worry about me at this point in the game. "Hey, no worries," I said. "I'll be OK."

There was a long pause in what was turning out to be a kind of uncomfortable conversation. "Coffee's good," I offered. "Thanks."

He waved my thanks away. "Heard your mom's got some problems," he said.

"Yeah, she does."

Frank's dad shook his head, was silent for a couple of minutes. I wasn't sure how much he knew or how much he wanted to know. It was always a judgment call, telling anybody about Mom, and inadvertently I winced as a mental image rushed through my mind of Mom fighting her way through those procedures that left her pale and trembling, gasping for breath. She would enter a sleep so deep afterwards, so exhausted, it sometimes seemed she'd left her body here and gone to another place altogether.

"She's pretty sick," I said finally.

"Cancer?"

He took a sip of coffee, his eyes focussed in on mine, and I nodded briefly, my head sunk down between my shoulders. "Yeah, well, they're not entirely sure how bad it is yet, but yeah, it's probably some kind of cancer."

He shook his head and gave me a sad kind of smile, then sat back. "Give me a buck, Rooster," he said.

"A buck?" This was unexpected. "Sure," I said. "For what?"

"No questions," he said with a short laugh. "So, have you got a dollar on you? One you can spare?"

For the first time since I'd got there, the man grinned at me with something like humour in his eyes. His cheeks were sunken but shaved clean, with a short growth of rusty goatee on his chin, and with that skinny face his resemblance to his dead son was uncanny. He wore an old plaid shirt with frayed cuffs over a pair of paint-splattered jeans and scuffed work boots. It seemed this might have been a sudden decision, asking me to meet for coffee, one that interrupted some work around the house or garage.

"Where's that loonie?" he persisted.

"Why do you want a dollar from me?" I was digging in my jeans for change. "You want a doughnut? I'll get us a couple if you want."

"Just give me the dollar, will ya?" Frank's dad grinned crookedly. "Quit arguing and hand one over."

Well, all right then. I dropped a loonie in his outstretched hand and he fished two fingers into his shirt pocket, pulled out a key ring and dropped it next to my cup.

"Here," he said with a gruff note in his voice. "Drive safe and take care of the old girl."

"What's this?"

"Car keys." He sipped at his cup, his eyes on the liquid. "Frank's Miata."

"You're giving me a car?" The keys sat there in a little heap by my cup, but I could only stare at them; I couldn't quite bring myself to pick them up. It was Frank's old key ring, the one with the army dog tags he'd found in a surplus store on it. "You're giving me Frank's car?"

"Not giving it to you!" Frank's dad's voice had that over the top, yo-ho quality to it like people get when they're trying to disguise sorrow with a false bravado. "I'm selling it to you! For a buck."

"Yeah, but sir," I began, "you don't need to do this."

"I know," he sighed and rubbed his hands over his cheeks and eyes. "I realize I don't have to do this, but I want to do this. I've been thinking about doing it for months, and then this morning I was rotating the tires on my car, putting the all-seasons back on since the snow's gone, and thinking I should do the same for Frank."

He looked out the window at the chilly spring wind blowing garbage around the parking lot and then finally turned back to me.

"It's crazy," he said. "I know it's crazy, but last fall I winterized his car. Put the winter tires on. Nobody drove it, of course, but it was ready to drive and now, I just figured, why was I keeping this car in the garage? Frank would want someone to enjoy it. He'd want you to enjoy it."

He paused for a second and his mouth kind of shook a little. He took a long sip of coffee, struggling to swallow and keep up the normal act. "He'd want you to drive it and look after it. Frank loved that old beater."

I knew he did. Frank had adored his wreck of a car. The thing was almost 20 years old, older than Frank had been when he died, and it was a glutton for attention. An ancient soft-top Miata, the paint so old and sunburned it's more orange than red, it runs about the way you'd expect a 20-year-old car to run. The car had been his uncle's when it was new, and when the uncle moved on to something else, the car started its slide down in the family ranks to a cousin and another nephew and then finally ended up as Frank's first car.

"Hold on, one second," I said. There was no way I could just sit there, watching Frank's dad try to act like this was a normal everyday transaction. I made my way to the counter, giving him a couple of minutes alone, and bought us a couple of muffins.

"Here, sir, my treat," I said, sitting down again. "And thanks. Thanks a lot for thinking of me."

My own voice was starting to give me away at that point, and Frank's dad was staring purposefully out the window again. We were both being men. Or trying to. Neither of us was willing to do a total meltdown in the middle of the local Tim's.

It's only a car, and I know that. Anyone can buy a car. But this one is one I've pushed when Frank ran out of gas. It's one we loafed around in and talked about taking road trips in when we got some money scraped up. We'd upgraded the music system together. It gives me a good reason to be in the garage, out of the house when I need to be, and it's something to look after and to tinker around with. Actually, it needs a fair bit of tinkering, but it's fast like shit out of a goose, even as old as it is.

Maybe it was the plain fact of having the Miata in our garage, of sitting in it for a while once I brought it home, and then driving it to school next day. Maybe it was some leftover Frank energy in the car, but another dream happened a couple of nights after I brought the car home.

This time I was bowling, and I was feeling good. Better than I've felt in ages. As good as I remember feeling back when I was a really little kid who used to wake up with all kinds of energy. So, I was really strong and happy, standing there in two-toned bowling shoes, with a big ball cupped in both my hands. The ball was a bright green thing, and my fingers around it were transparent—long, and knobby at the knuckles like they are in real life, but see-through. Everything around me was vibrant and almost throbbing with colour. I could *hear* the colours, that's how strong they were.

A long, long lane stretched out in front of me, with little white pins way down at the end, and I stood there poised, ready to aim that ball right down the centre of it. Then, as I narrowed my eyes and aimed, the lane developed a white centre line like a highway and the pins at the end disappeared in a misty fog. The track was now a lot longer than any bowling lane in any alley in the world, with deep gutters at both sides, almost as deep as ravines or valleys, filled with wildflowers, blowing around like crazy. And the thing was wide, widening as it went, until it dominated the landscape. That lane ran so far into the distance that it finally turned into a curving wooded passageway with 10 fir trees, instead of the pins, standing there at the end like dark-green sentinels.

There were shadows all around me, but not on the ground like shadows normally are. Instead, they were all through the air. They were shadows that didn't seem to be representative of anything else that was there, but they ebbed and flowed and broke into other shadows. There were shadows upon shadows, and they left a soft feeling behind. I could feel myself climbing and slipping through layers of warm, soft consciousness, that gigantic bowling ball still clutched in my hands.

And then suddenly Frank was beside me, bowling, too, turning to laugh at me. In his hands was a bowling ball, bright yellow, that when he turned to throw it down the lane, became unwound into a long wide shining ribbon, which in turn unfurled into a bird. The flapping bird soared out of his hands; a brilliant yellow creature sailing with wings outspread down that bowling alley, which had become a country lane. And I woke up with a smile on my face, thinking of Ari and how much she was going to enjoy me telling her about this latest development.

26

Early the following October, a year and a half after they died, I drove the Miata up through the mountains, past the Jasper town site and along the Jasper-Banff parkway, and I did it alone. With me I had a good sleeping bag, a mediocre tent and some dried and canned foods and, although there had been a few people who'd volunteered to come along, I'd insisted on completing this trek by myself.

The pine and spruce trees were clusters of dark green, the way they'd stay all through the seasons, but the birch stands, both in the valleys and those higher up the mountain sides, had turned a bright yellow, shining in brilliant patches in the thin autumn sunlight. The leaves on the smaller bushes, the wild raspberries, willows, roses and bunchberries, were red, turning slowly to brown, and ready to start dropping, leaving the branches bare for winter. With the tourists mostly gone for the season, it was gorgeous up there in the low mountain passes—remote, still and silent.

The little exit off the highway wasn't hard to find, even though I hadn't been there in a couple of years, and the wobbly gate and short drive in to an almost-hidden little parking area were as deserted as they usually are. It had been one reason Frank and I loved the place so much. There was never much of a chance of running into anyone else in the parking place, let alone up by the lake and in the meadows beyond that. The tiny wooden-framed hostel at Mosquito Lake was closed for the season, so there weren't even any backpackers or hitchhikers nearby. I pulled the car into the space farthest in from the highway, pulled on hiking boots and a jacket and yanked my old backpack out of the passenger seat. I locked the car up, before taking stock of what lay in front of me.

It took only a little searching through underbrush to find the narrow trailhead leading up to Marion Lake. The path was marked by the same weathered wooden sign, tilted behind a bank of overgrown browning ferns. The same place where Frank and I had found it a year before the snowslide. I pulled the backpack straps over my shoulders, settled the weight of tent and sleeping bag to a comfortable level, parted the bushes and started walking.

The first snows had already dropped their load down the flanks of the mountains, whitening the valleys and dusting the trees like a coating of icing sugar. Nights were now below freezing, even in the lower elevations, but the daytime highs in the valleys were warm enough still to keep life comfortable. The higher up the mountains a person walked, the colder it would become, so that even if the sun came out the temperature on those granite heights up around Marion Lake would hover close enough to freezing to maintain the first skiffs of snow all day. Making the contrast of pure white snow against the steel grey of stone and deep green of the fir trees a beautiful sight.

Staring up to the peaks above as I walked, I knew there'd only be a couple of hours of daylight left to me, but that was enough to get me up to where they'd spent their final nights and I was comfortable going there on my own. Bear-bells on my backpack were jingling, but bears were not much of a concern at this point. I figured the animals would be high up in the backcountry looking for winter dens and getting pretty sleepy already. Mom had insisted, though, and the bells were there, keeping me company.

For the longest time my greatest wish had been that I'd gone with them. Dying alongside Frank and Jen had seemed an easier fate than living without them. Those days were mostly behind me now, but there was still the feeling in my gut of being so alone, so empty in this world, that my stomach sometimes felt like it was going to sink out of sight like a stone tossed in a pond.

Their memories had faded into something warmer, less devastating, than before, but still potent. This trip was a way of marking how much they'd meant to me in their lives, how much they still meant to me, and how far I'd come personally since their deaths. It was important to me to do something to mark their passing and important that the thing I chose to do had meaning for me, if not for anyone else. I had thought long and deep about what I needed to do and the plan I finally came up with was to simply go there. The idea was to hike up the mountain, and camp as near to where they'd had their tent as I could find. It was a simple plan, but it worked for me and the main component of it was to not do anything that felt fake.

So, here's what I did not do. I didn't put a memorial cross up in the ditch on the highway close to the turn-off for everyone driving by to see and wonder who it was there for. I didn't write their names on the granite walls at the side of the road or deface the mountains in any way. I didn't drop flowers where they'd camped or scatter their ashes in the half-frozen lake. I didn't say a prayer or build a stone cairn to their memory. I only climbed up through that first light, dry snow of the season, breathing in the crisp fall air, and when I got to the flat little meadow where their empty campsite had been found, I pitched my dome tent on a flat piece of ground under a tall spruce.

The waters of Marion Lake were choppy and cold with little chunks of slushy ice when I finally reached them. Winter was on its way. Wandering around near the lakeside, I gathered a dozen flat rocks and laid them in a rough circle on a small patch of dirt near my tent. I scouted through the brush for dry twigs, pine needles, grass and deadfall for a fire. Gathering up an armful of dried fallen branches and with a handful of splintery winter grass, I laid the little grasses in a small pyramid, with a few thin sticks holding them in place, then lit a match and blew gently on the tiny flames, adding more wood as the fire grew in size and strength. Filling my kettle with lakewater for tea, I boiled the water for a solid five minutes, before spiking my cup with teaspoons of sugar. Then I sat back with my hot sweet tea and let the aching emptiness settle inside me in the twilight of that first night.

I'd brought two books, shoving them deep into my backpack before I left home, so once the tent was up and camp was made, I dug them out again from where they were tucked under my spare jeans and socks, way at the bottom of the pack. They'd both kind of jumped off a shelf at me in a second-hand bookstore months earlier. The first was an account written by a guy who'd been rescued from an avalanche years earlier, describing how it had happened and what he'd done and felt before he'd been dug out. The second was a textbook type of thing explaining what happened to people caught in avalanches in more scientific, less personal, terms. It described human bodies and the automatic coping mechanisms that would kick in once they'd been buried and before they'd died.

In the flickering light provided by the fire, I flipped on my flashlight and leafed through each book, reading in spurts and then closing them in order to lay more wood on the fire or stir up another pot of tea. There was no rush. I had all night and nobody else to consider and I sat there for hours, watching the night sky brighten up with thousands of stars, while the sparks from my fire swirled up and got caught in the little breeze.

Ice masks form when a person's caught by a snowslide. Ice masks form around faces when they get buried. Sometimes there's a half-hour of breathing time, if the person had the chance to throw an arm over his head and maybe carve a little facial cave in the snow. It's dark. There's nothing to see. When the snow pack falls, it goes fast. Really fast, and there's no way of outrunning it or out-skiing it if the person's directly in the path of the thing.

Then, when the avalanche stops, the slabs of snow settle like heavy concrete. Any kind of movement is nearly impossible, so Frank and Jen were trapped with their arms and legs pinned in whatever position they'd held when the snow stopped moving, unable to dig or push at the stuff. They waited. Maybe they hoped, and maybe they didn't. They might have been unconscious. They would have been tumbled around like puppets in the turmoil of the falling snow shelves and so they wouldn't have known which direction was up anymore. Their bodies weren't dug out for over 24 hours after the slide, so they would not have survived even if they'd been able to move an arm and dig a bigger cave in front of their faces. Their breathable air would have run out.

When the snow comes sliding down it becomes icy, because the friction of the slide makes the temperature of the snow drop and then when it's around a face, a living, breathing warm face, it forms condensation and it freezes hard. Real hard. So then in addition to being pinned and unable to dig, a person would have a helluva time breaking through the ice that formed in a cave around their face even if they had one hand free to dig or scratch at it.

There was no room for debate on knowing that Frank and Jen, if they'd survived the initial plunge down the mountain, would have been helpless, trapped in complete darkness. The pressure of the snow on their chests and the rest of their bodies would have felt like a ton of solid weight, bearing down on their bones and muscles, hurting their bodies and making their breathing a life-and-death struggle. Then the air would have eventually run out for them and they would have smothered.

I could only read these facts in little bursts, taking a break every few minutes and stirring up my fire, trying to not lose my sometimes faint grip on who I was and where I was in my own life. It wasn't possible for me to live that horrifying experience for them, but I needed to understand and break it down into its components, respect they'd lived it alone and I had not, and then I had to let it go.

I camped in that place for two nights—one for each of them, or at least that's how I reasoned it out in my head.

The first night was long and dark, thankfully without dreams. Next morning, I woke early to the sight of sun warming the sides of my tent. I boiled water and cooked up a pot of hot oatmeal, then packed a little day-pack with granola bars and chocolate, tossing in a bottle of water from home and extra socks in case the ones I had on got wet or wore through someplace. It's best, I've found, to try to anticipate discomfort or potential issues and then sidestep them if possible, especially out camping where there's nobody to depend on but yourself. Best to keep your brains about you, and that's what I intended to do. This expedition was not about becoming all wrought up or indulging in self-blame; this expedition was just to mark their having been here. It was a way of joining them, since I'd missed out on the first trip. A way of keeping us a team.

Once around the other side of the lake, all I needed to do was follow a small stream-bed and then cross over it to climb higher. The path up the mountain was fairly steep, but reasonably trail-worthy. Obviously used by animals, probably mountain sheep and deer. Frank and Jen wouldn't have seen the trail, since they were here when the snow was probably 10 feet deep, but I followed it anyway. It was easy, once I'd climbed a little farther, to see where they'd been skiing, since although the snow from the avalanche had melted long ago, it had left a long destructive swath of trees damaged from its powerful surge that was still obvious even months later.

Broken off and jagged-edged spruce and pine trees were scrambled in a wild mish-mash of straight barren posts, piled one over another like toothpicks. Needles and dried dead branches were tossed around, piled on the rocky terrain left by the avalanche's massive churning. Other trees, the younger, more malleable ones towards the bottom of the slide, remained bent over, but still alive and leafy yet from the summer, looking as if something heavy had sat on them hard enough to bend but not break. It seemed like they were bowing down the mountainside. Bowing to some superior power.

That night when I finished the canned chili I'd brought along, I put the books away, and sat there, my hands resting on my knees, watching the moon change colour on its revolution through the night sky. One more night. I'd be leaving the next morning, and I doubted I'd ever return. There were other places to camp and I'd find them over the years, but this one place was sacred to me and I intended to respect its isolation.

The fire I built that night ribboned out around the smaller logs, little licks biting into the dried bark and then finally evolving into becoming the deeper fire, inside the heart of the logs themselves. They glowed red-hot, the chunks of wood breaking down into black, grey, and deep red-purple coals. Flames slithered around each other, rising in the dark, sending sparks flying out over the chill of the evening, slipping through and around the firewood.

Getting up from the log I'd been sitting on, I stretched my legs out and walked down to the lake to splash some cold water over my face. I stared out across the silent black waters, then wandered a bit through the underbrush and picked up some more deadfall for the fire. Circling the fire, I placed my logs like a teepee where they were needed, building the flames up into a pyramid of yellow and red.

And then, acting on what must have been a primitive impulse, I started a sort of crazy dance. There was nobody there to see me, but still at first I hopped a little tentatively, skipping from one foot to the other, but being quiet about it as if I was afraid someone might be hiding in the bushes ready to laugh at me. The more I moved around the fire, though, the less inhibited I became. I was waving my arms by then and jumping around, turning and weaving, running a little and circling the firepit. An owl swooped past me, silent and heavily weightless, like a shadow, and I bent at the waist and mimicked his flight, my arms out at my sides like a bird.

I threw my head back and let go a little howl, then got braver and yowled louder. I yelled. I screamed. Tears rolled down my face without my even knowing they were there, wetting my cheeks and neck, and I wiped wildly at the gluey mess of snot and tears covering my face. My hair clung to my head, sweaty from the heat thrown off by the fire and by my exertions. Hollering, I swirled and turned, faster and faster, around that flickering bonfire, shrieking my pain to the night sky.

The fire was huge by this point, licking up in a frenzy of flame and fuel, and I stripped off my jacket, tossing it towards the tent, then threw my shirt after it. Bare-chested, I ran as fast as I could round and round the flames, then stopped, panting, and kicked my boots and pants off into a heap.

Leaping naked around the fire, my head back, my arms waving and legs shaking with the effort of the rage and the passion being released, I danced there in the moonlight, all alone, screaming my agony and my sorrow until my throat was raw.

I don't know how long I continued this frantic swirling dance, this painful outpouring, but finally I found myself in my tent, in my sleeping bag, my eyes half-closed and quiet. Resting. Listening to the small sounds of the world in the woods outside and feeling a sense of peace.

That night was dreamless once again, for which I was thankful, but there was a point just as the sun was starting to light up the sides of the tent, while I was only semi-awake, when I felt a little hand creep into mine. Slim fingers, warm and alive, curled into my fingers, wrapping themselves around and holding me. Jen's slender, elegant fingers squeezed me tight and there for one split second her hand was in mine.